The last thing Callum expected to find while out flying was a van full of kidnapped people. He has no idea what to do with them, but thankfully, they're not his problem for long.

His mate is.

When Moore sends Leon to rescue a group of kidnapped people, he expects to fight hunters, not to meet his mate. He's spent years staying away from his family to make sure the hunters wouldn't find them, but he's not sure he can do the same when it comes to Callum.

Callum won't be kept away, and Leon has to accept that. Can he, or will he give in to the fear that something will happen to his mate — and that it will be his fault?

Leon
Copyright © 2023 Catherine Lievens
ISBN: 978-1-4874-3913-2
Cover art by Angela Waters

Published by eXtasy Books Inc

Look for us online at:
www.eXtasybooks.com

LEON
MUTANTS 4

BY

CATHERINE LIEVENS

CHAPTER ONE

Hayes kept peeking at the diner's door. Normally, Leon wouldn't have thought anything about it, but he couldn't help but tease his friend.

"Aren't you supposed to know when Rikar's coming? I mean, the two of you are bonded, and he's a Nix. Surely, you can reach out to him and ask him where he is."

Hayes glared, but he didn't look angry. "I don't want to bother him. He's working."

As the leader of their small village and tribe, Rikar had plenty of work to do, and Leon didn't envy him. He could only imagine how annoying it was to deal with so many people and complaints on a daily basis. It was a miracle Rikar hadn't run out of the village screaming and promising he'd never be back. Leon was pretty sure that was what he'd have done if he'd been in Rikar's place.

But Rikar wasn't shouldering this on his own anymore. He had Hayes, and while Hayes was uncomfortable with being called anything more than a mutant, there was no denying that he was becoming a central part of the village. When Rikar wasn't available, people went to Hayes, and he was going on fewer missions as time passed.

Leon didn't mind. He didn't want any of his friends to be in danger, so it was good that Hayes had decided to start staying back. He still went when Moore needed him, but Moore had noticed what was happening, or rather, his mate had pointed it out. Jolyn had suggested that Moore give Hayes and Rikar time and space for their relationship to grow. That

1

meant doing without Hayes when they were on raids, so sometimes it wasn't easy, but they made it work. They would all do whatever it took to ensure their fellow mutants were happy, no matter what it meant for the mission.

Leon leaned back against the bench and took a sip of his soda. He still believed in the cause that pushed them to fight back against the people who'd hurt them so badly. Like all the other mutants, Leon had been through hell, and he'd come out of it changed and convinced of what their team was doing.

He wished he hadn't had to live through all of that, but he couldn't deny he didn't have a problem with how he'd been changed. Before, he'd been nothing more than a shifter, and while that was fine, he wouldn't have been able to do what he did now if he'd remained simply a shifter. As it was, he could heal people, which gave him more satisfaction than anything else he could have done with his life.

"If he's working, aren't you supposed to be working with him?" Teddy teased, winking at Leon as he did so.

Hayes's glare deepened, but now it was aimed at Teddy. "I'm not Rikar's beta. I'm not a co-mayor or whatever you want to call it. I have nothing to do with his job as this village's leader."

"Keep telling yourself that," Davey muttered around his burger.

Leon snickered. It was fun to tease Hayes, but none of them wanted their friend to get angry. Besides, if Hayes would rather not think about how he was becoming a pride leader, Leon wasn't going to burst his bubble.

Hayes needed time. He and Rikar hadn't been together that long, and it had been a massive adjustment. Hayes wasn't just a follower anymore. No matter what he thought or what he wanted to think, the fact that he was Rikar's mate meant that he couldn't get out of becoming a prominent figure in the village.

"You know, you've been teasing me mercilessly about finding my mate, but you're going to eventually, and when you do, my time will come." Hayes grinned evilly and steepled his fingers together. "I'm going to have so much fun."

Leon snorted. "Just because you found your mate doesn't mean we will. It doesn't work that way."

"Doesn't it? Because from what I've seen, when people start meeting their mates, the rest of their family and friends do shortly after."

Leon didn't want to believe that. He wouldn't know what to do with a mate, and more importantly, he was unwilling to put anyone in danger. Considering what he and the other mutants did for a living, it would be too easy for the people they cared about to be hurt. Besides, the hunters weren't the mutants' only enemies. They also had to be careful of the council, the council assassins, the people who worked in the labs, and the hunters.

Leon couldn't believe that he'd once thought the labs were part of the past. He'd thought shifters were safe, but he couldn't have been more wrong, and he'd paid for that. He'd been turned into a mutant, something not quite shifter anymore, and it had taken him a long time to wrap his mind around that. He'd lost everything and wasn't about to put himself and his heart in that position ever again. No, it was better if he never met his mate. That way, when he lost them, he wouldn't be hurt. Hell, he wouldn't even know he'd lost them.

But not everyone felt like he did when it came to mates. Teddy sighed, and his expression turned dopey. "I can't wait."

Leon snorted. He didn't say anything, but Teddy frowned anyway.

"What? I can't want to find my mate? To finally have one

who will love me for who I am and won't demand things I can't give them?" Teddy asked.

Leon didn't want to fight with any of his best friends. Besides, he understood what Teddy was talking about. It just wasn't for him. "Of course you can. If that's what you want, I hope you'll find your mate as soon as possible, maybe even today or tomorrow."

"I hope you'll all find your mates," Hayes interjected.

Leon could feel him watching him. He had no doubt that his friend had realized he wasn't as enthusiastic about meeting his mate as Teddy. They'd never talked about it, but Hayes knew Leon better than Leon knew himself sometimes.

Leon shook his head. "I don't want to meet my mate."

"Why not? Please tell me it's not because you think you don't deserve it or something like that."

"There's so much danger. We're still fighting hunters and raiding labs, and I don't want to bring anyone I care about into this life."

"But they're already in this life, even if they don't know it. Even if they're humans, the hunters are taking whoever they can get their hands on. They prefer shifters, but it doesn't mean humans are safe."

Leon was aware of that, which made everything even scarier. It would have been bad enough if his mate turned out to be a shifter. What if they were human?

That wasn't something he wanted to think about, or even worse, talk about. "Well, whoever my mate is, they can stay away. I'm too busy right now."

While that was the truth, Leon couldn't deny that what Teddy yearned for was appealing. He only had to look at Hayes and Rikar to know that if he met his mate, he'd probably be happier than he'd ever been. To have that special someone who could understand him without words and love him in a way no one else could was enough to make Leon dream.

But he'd left his family behind for a reason. He had never contacted them, even after he'd been freed from the lab. They probably thought he was dead, and he didn't want to hurt them any more than they already had been. More importantly, considering his job, he didn't want to put them in danger. It would be too easy for them to be sucked into this life, and Leon would hate himself if that happened.

So he'd make sure it didn't. If that meant staying away from his family, that was what he'd do. It wasn't easy, and some days, it was hard to resist the temptation, but it was the right thing to do.

No matter how much he wanted trust, love, and closeness, he couldn't do it, not when it would put the people most important to him in danger.

There was nothing Callum enjoyed more than flying, so it was a good thing that he was a bat shifter. He didn't know what he would have done if he'd been another kind of shifter. Well, maybe he wouldn't have loved flying as much as he did. It didn't matter, because he *was* a bat shifter, and he could fly anytime he wanted.

Which was what he was doing at the moment. He swooped lower, flying just above his dog's head. Maxim barked and tried to catch him, and Callum flew higher. His dog would never hurt him. They'd been playing like this since Maxim was a puppy, and he'd learned that Callum was still Callum, even when he was in his bat form. Callum trusted him with his life.

It was almost time to head home to feed the dog and maybe even himself. Callum wasn't often hungry when he should be, but he was always up for some fruit, so maybe he'd have that for dinner. It was tempting, and his stomach growled as he thought of the watermelon in his fridge.

Okay, maybe he *was* hungry.

He swooped into the air, ready to turn back, when a loud crash startled him. He hesitated for a moment, knowing he shouldn't get involved. He and Max had been playing close to a road, but they usually stayed away from it, even though it wasn't busy. Only locals took it, which meant that whatever had happened probably involved someone who lived in the area. That didn't mean Callum should be involved, but he didn't think he could leave knowing someone might be hurt. What would happen if they needed medical help? Could Callum really stay away?

He looked down at his dog. His first priority would always be Max, but maybe Callum could go there, find out what happened, and get someone to help. He didn't have to be involved any more than that.

Hopefully.

He sighed and flew toward the area where he'd heard the sound come from. When he reached the road, he glanced around, trying to find the accident. He had no doubt that was what happened, but he couldn't imagine how anyone would have had an accident on this road unless a wild animal was involved. He could see the red lights at the back of a vehicle in the ditch by the road, and he quickly flew there, Max following him on the ground.

The van was white and looked like any other van. It was tilted forward, and it would be a pain in the ass to pull out. That wouldn't be Callum's problem, though. No, Callum's problem was finding out if the driver was all right.

Before Callum could make any kind of decision, Max stopped by the back of the truck and started pawing at the door. Callum tried to distract him by flying over his head, but Max was stubborn. When he wanted something, he stared at Callum until Callum gave in, and if he didn't, he pouted and made Callum feel guilty.

It seemed like tonight would be one of those nights.

But Callum had to check on the driver, no matter what had caught Max's attention at the back of the van. Because of the vehicle's position, he wouldn't be able to do much in this form. That meant he had to shift, something he wasn't eager to do since he'd be naked when he did. But it was either that or leaving the driver where they were, and Callum would never forgive himself if they were in pain or wounded.

He huffed.

Since there was no getting out of it, he shifted to his naked human form, wrapping his arms around himself as soon as he did. The beginning of November was way too cold for him to do something like this. The problem was that in his bat form, he was small, which meant he couldn't carry a bag around his neck like some of the bigger shifters did. No, when he went flying, he could only bring himself, which at the moment was a problem because he didn't have clothes.

The sooner he found the driver, the sooner he could shift back and go home. He moved around the van, trying to get to the driver's door, but it was blocked by a tree and a bunch of bushes. He had to walk around the van to the passenger door.

"Is there anyone there?" he called out.

He expected the answer to come from the driver's side of the van, but instead, someone started screaming from the back of it. Callum stared, trying to wrap his mind around what that meant.

He could hear several voices, and all of them were calling for help. Why were at least three people stuck in the back of this van? It couldn't be good, and while Callum had no idea what he'd stumbled onto, it wasn't going to make him back down. Whoever was stuck in the back of the van needed his help, and he would provide it.

He couldn't leave, no matter how much he wanted to and how little he wanted to be involved in whatever this messy situation was. It might take hours before someone else drove down the road, and anything could happen in the meantime.

With a heavy sigh, he peeked through the passenger's side window. He grimaced at the sight of the driver slumped sideways, pressed between the airbag and the driver's door, blood dripping down his forehead. The dumb ass hadn't worn his seatbelt, and while the airbag had deployed, there was no way to know if it had been useful.

Callum tried knocking on the door, but the driver didn't wake up. Callum carefully opened the door. If the guy woke up now, he'd understand Callum was trying to help, right?

Callum tried to ignore the voices coming from the back of the van and quickly scrambled onto the seat, trying to ignore the blood. His fingers shook as he reached for the man's neck to find a pulse. No matter how hard he focused, he couldn't find anything. The voices coming from the back of the van didn't make it any easier.

The guy was dead, which meant there was nothing Callum could do for him. He got out and then turned his attention to the people in the back. He had no idea what was happening in there, but he still couldn't leave.

"Hello?" he called out.

"Hello?" a voice answered. "Can you hear me?"

"Yeah. Is everyone in there all right?"

There was a pause before the voice answered. "Not really."

That wasn't what Callum had hoped to hear. "Is someone hurt?"

"Yeah. We need help."

The voice was masculine, but Callum could hear at least one woman as well. "I can see if the driver has the key," he offered. "I'll also call nine-one-one."

"Wait," the man who'd been talking to him said. "You can't call nine-one-one."

"You said someone's hurt," Callum pointed out.

"Please. I have a phone number. If you could call them, they'll come and help us and make sure the hunters can't take us again."

Callum blinked. Hunters? What was this guy talking about? "Fine. I'll call whoever you want, but give me a moment to find the keys first."

Swallowing, he went to the passenger door. He scrambled back into the van, holding his breath as if he expected the driver to have moved. He didn't—the man was very much dead, and he didn't react even when Callum turned off the engine and slid the key out of the ignition. He quickly moved back, unwilling to spend even one more second in there with a dead body. He didn't care that dead bodies couldn't hurt him. He'd watched way too many zombie movies to know that wasn't the case.

Once he was at the back of the van again, he had to find a way to get to the lock. That meant he had to climb up, since the van was tilted into the ditch, which wasn't the greatest thing to do while he was naked and freezing his ass off. As soon as the key was in the lock, he turned it, relieved when it did what it was supposed to do. He opened the doors, then quickly hopped down, just in case. Max came to sit by his feet, and together, they watched as a man appeared.

The man was hesitant. Callum waved at him, unsure what to do. The man blinked, turned, and held a hand out to whoever else was in the van.

This time, a woman came out. Callum reached for his phone to call nine-one-one or whoever this guy wanted to call, only to swear when he realized he was freaking naked and didn't have his phone with him.

He eyed the front of the van. He was going to have to steal the dead man's phone, wasn't he?

When the diner door opened and Moore appeared, Leon knew from his expression that he wasn't going to like whatever his boss had to say. He straightened, watching Moore as he came closer. He seemed to know exactly where to find them, which was probably the case. The village was small, and it wasn't like they'd been hiding.

Leon wasn't the only one who noticed Moore. Teddy looked up, grimaced, then tilted his chin toward Moore to let Davey and Hayes know he was there.

"Hey," Moore said as he reached them.

Hayes groaned. "Let me guess. Another rescue mission?"

"Always," Moore said with a smile. "I don't need all of you, just Teddy and Leon."

Teddy and Leon looked at each other. Teddy and Leon were almost always present during the raids. Teddy was a Nix, which meant that his shimmering ability was enough to warrant his presence there, while Leon could heal many more problems than even Nix healers could. He was always on standby, ready to help their friends or the people they found trapped in the labs. The fact that Moore only wanted the two of them meant the mission wouldn't be big, but that they'd need an easy way in and out and that someone was probably hurt.

"What happened?" Leon asked as he got to his feet.

"Got a weird phone call at the number Rikar's been handing out for us," Moore explained. "This guy said that he found a crashed van on the side of the road and that one of the people locked in the back of the van told him to call that number."

"Locked?" Teddy asked.

Moore nodded. "The guy doesn't know anything as far as I can tell, but yeah. He said he found a bunch of people just locked in the van. The driver's dead, and there wasn't anyone else there, so he has no idea what to do or what happened."

"Are we sure it's not a trap?" Leon asked.

"We can never be sure of that, but I don't think so. The guy who called, Callum, said he's a shifter. He was playing around with his dog when he heard the crash and the screams. From what he said, the road isn't busy, so we shouldn't have a problem getting to the van and helping those people."

Part of what Moore was saying was good, but Leon was still worried. "The driver?"

"Dead. There isn't anyone else, so we should be fine."

"It's that *should* that worries me," Teddy muttered,

Leon couldn't blame him. Unfortunately, They wouldn't know the situation until they got there.

"I'll call you later," Leon promised after he turned to Hayes and Davey.

"We'll want all the details," Davey warned him.

That wouldn't be a problem. When it came to these missions, every mutant knew what happened, even when they weren't in on it. They had to know what was happening in the world around them, especially regarding the hunters and the people they hurt.

Leon wasn't sure what was worse — the hunters who captured humans and shifters to take them to the labs, or the scientists who gleefully hurt those people by experimenting on them and modifying their DNA. Hadn't they already done enough harm? They knew how to do that stuff because they'd been doing it for decades. Leon was the result of one of those experiments, as were his closest friends and other mutants. He still didn't know what the scientists were trying to do, and he was starting to think that for most of them, it was just work. They wanted to find out more about how shifters and humans worked and how they could change them, and they didn't have a goal beyond satisfying their curiosity.

The thought made him want to throw up.

Leon, Teddy, and Moore left the diner. It was getting late,

but there were still people around, walking down the sidewalks. The village was peaceful, and Leon was happy he'd found a home here. He'd had no hope he and the other mutants ever would after they'd been changed, but even though they were different, they'd found a place for to call home. He would never leave this place.

"Where to?" Teddy asked.

"The guy on the phone sent a picture of the van and the people inside it. You can focus on that, right?" Moore asked as he took his phone out.

"Of course." Teddy held out his hand.

Moore took it while Leon grabbed Teddy's shoulder. He tried to empty his mind so he wouldn't hinder the shimmering while Moore showed Teddy the picture on his phone. Teddy stared for a moment before nodding, and they were gone before Leon could think too hard about it.

They appeared on the side of a small road. The night was dark, and Leon almost didn't see the group of people standing by the crashed van in front of them.

Moore swore. "This is going to be a mess. We need light."

"I'm going back to grab flashlights," Teddy said.

"Find Matthew, too."

Teddy grinned and vanished. Matthew's mutant power dealt with electricity. When he needed to, he could light himself up like a lamp. He didn't like doing it, because people always made fun of him, but he'd be useful in this situation, although Leon hoped they wouldn't have to stick around too long. He didn't like this place and didn't think he was the only one who felt that way.

He and Moore were cautious as they approached the group around the van. They both used their phone flashlights to see where they were going, and by the time they reached the van, Leon had counted five people huddled together.

"I'm Moore," Moore declared. "Can anyone tell me what

happened?"

The five looked at each other. It was clear they were frightened, and Leon didn't blame them. He didn't know what had happened for sure, but he could imagine that they'd all been taken by the hunters and that the van had crashed while they were on their way to a lab. That meant there was a lab nearby, and he couldn't stop himself from looking around to find it. They'd need to raid it soon, but right now, their focus had to be on the survivors.

"You're the leader of the mutants," one of the men said.

Moore rubbed the back of his neck. "I try. Can anyone tell me what happened? Is anyone hurt?"

"The driver hit Amy," the man said, gently pushing a woman forward.

Leon raised his phone, wincing at the bruise on the woman's face. He stepped closer, not surprised when she stepped back. He raised his hands, wanting her to know he wasn't going to hurt her.

"I'm just going to heal you."

Amy didn't seem convinced, but she nodded and allowed Leon to move closer again. It was just a bruise, nothing he wasn't used to healing, so he was done after just a few seconds.

Once the others saw what he could do, they came closer willingly. He didn't have much to heal, just a few bruises and scrapes, but he worried about how dehydrated some of these people were. Thankfully, Teddy was back quickly.

Leon looked around, but there was nothing else for him to do. His gaze caught on a naked guy standing next to the van, a dog sitting by his feet. Leon frowned, wondering what had happened to this guy. Moore had mentioned that the guy who'd found these people was a shifter, but Leon hadn't expected to see him naked. It was cold, and he was worried about the man.

He moved toward him. "Hey," he said, smiling in what he hoped was a reassuring gesture. "I'm Leon. I'm a healer, so if you're hurt, I can help you."

The man shuffled his feet. "I'm fine."

"I'm pretty sure your lips are blue, so I don't think you are."

"I'll be fine as soon as I shift back. I just wanted to make sure everyone was all right and that you didn't have any questions for me."

"We have plenty of questions, but you don't have to stand there naked while you wait. Why don't you shift back until we're ready for you?"

"I would like to go home, actually. It's getting late."

Leon stopped in front of the man. He was cute, and keeping his focus on the man's face wasn't easy. Leon was tempted to look down but told himself he couldn't. It wouldn't be fair to the man, who'd only been trying to help these people.

"I'm Leon," he said, holding out his hand.

The man stared for a moment before taking it. "Callum."

Callum was slightly shorter than Leon and plumper. His dark hair was long and braided, and the focus of his dark eyes jumped from Leon to the people still waiting for Teddy to return. He was incredibly handsome.

And he was Leon's mate.

The sexy man let go of Callum's hand as if it had burned him, and for a moment, Callum didn't understand what had happened. Had he been ogling Leon so much that Leon had noticed? Even if that was so, who would blame him?

Leon was tall and handsome, with brown curls and brown eyes. Callum could see that because of how incredibly *bright* one of the guys who apparently worked with Leon was. There was no way he was a normal shifter, and he definitely wasn't

14

human, but while Callum was curious about him, he was even more curious about Leon.

Especially when the wind shifted and he realized why Leon had dropped his hand.

Callum beamed as Leon's scent hit him. His brain was having a hard time with the news that his mate was standing in front of him, but he couldn't help but smile.

He'd found his mate.

Callum was excited, like any shifter would be. His mate was the one person who would complete him, who would be by his side for the rest of his life, who would love him and make him happy.

Except that might not be the case, because Leon didn't look as happy about this as Callum. He wasn't even smiling.

"So," Callum said.

"I have to go," Leon answered as he turned.

"Wait, please. I know you're in shock. So am I. I just don't want either of us to do something we'll regret, like running away before we talk." Callum needed Leon to stay where he was. He looked down, smiling when he saw that Max was still there. "This is my dog. His name is Maxime, although I usually call him Max." Among other things. Leon didn't need to be overwhelmed by all of Max's cute nicknames.

"I don't know what to say about any of this," Leon said.

"Neither do I."

"It looks to me like you know exactly what to say. You seem happy."

Callum beamed. "Of course I'm happy. I met you. I won't say I've been looking for you or whatever, but I've always wondered what you'd be like, and now, I know." He was perfect, or at least perfect for Callum, and that was all Callum cared about. Whatever problems they would have, they'd find a way to fix them. They were destined to be together.

Leon continued staring until Callum felt uncomfortable.

He was very much aware of the fact that he was completely naked, but unless he wanted to shift back, there was nothing he could do about that.

"So what are you guys? Why did the guy in the van call you guys? He was serious about me not calling nine-one-one."

Leon cleared his throat. "We're a group of people who help others."

"That tells me pretty much nothing," Callum teased. "You make it sound like you're some kind of superhero, like in the movies."

Leon spluttered. "We're not superheroes."

"I know that. No one is. You sure came in like a superhero, though. You didn't know what happened, but you still came for these people and healed them. I saw you."

Leon shrugged. "That's what I do. It's what *we* do."

"So you're what? A supersecret group? You can't tell me anything else because you'll have to kill me if you do?" Callum hoped that wasn't true. He didn't want to die, especially not right after meeting Leon.

"We're mutants."

Leon stared at Callum as if he expected him to be frightened by that revelation. Callum wasn't sure what Leon meant, but he wouldn't care even if Leon was a purple cow. Leon was his mate. He'd never hurt him. "All right. Can you tell me more about that?"

Leon blinked. "That's all you have to say about it?"

"What do you want me to say? I don't know what you mean, so I need more information."

"You're not scared?"

"Why would I be scared?"

Leon threw his hands in the air. "Maybe because I told you I'm a mutant?"

"Does that mean you can transform into a massive green

guy?" Green guy, purple cow, all of that was the same for Callum.

"I can't. My power is healing. I can heal anything, from a wound to an illness."

"That sounds great. Is that why your friend is lit like a Christmas tree?"

"Yes. His power deals with electricity."

Callum bounced on the balls of his feet. He was still really fucking cold, but he was too excited to care, or at least, he would be until he lost a toe or, worse, his balls. He suspected that if he shifted and headed home to grab his things, Leon would vanish, and he couldn't allow that to happen. He needed a location where he could find Leon or, even better, a phone number at the very least. Hell, he'd even take an email address at this point.

"Cool, so you're a mutant and can heal people. Your friend is a lightbulb. Are there more of you? What about the two guys who came with you?"

Leon shook his head, but there was a small smile on his lips. "We're all mutants. I don't understand why you're taking this so easily."

"How else should I take it? Do you want me to worry? Be afraid of you? Because I'm not, and I don't feel I have to be. You're here to help these people, and since I didn't do anything to them, it means I'm safe. As for the fact that you're a mutant, it doesn't matter, because you're my mate."

The words seemed to give Leon a jolt, as if he'd forgotten they were mates. Callum doubted he had. For him, it was impossible to ignore how delicious Leon smelled. He couldn't believe how lucky he'd been. Not only was Leon incredibly sexy, but he also helped people for a living. He had expected Callum to be afraid of him, but Callum couldn't care less about this mutant thing. Honestly, it was the least interesting thing about Leon.

"So, where do you live?"

"You get straight to the point."

"Why shouldn't I? I'm going to move there soon."

Once again, Leon blinked as if he hadn't expected Callum to say that. "Why would you move there?"

"Because you're my mate, and since you're part of this supersecret mutant group, I don't think you'll want to move. Besides, there's nothing keeping me here. I like the place just fine, but it's not where my mate is."

Was he coming on too strong? Probably, but if he and Leon were going to end up together, Leon probably should know that Callum was kind of impulsive. This wasn't something he'd regret, though. He wanted to be with Leon, and moving closer to him was the only way to make that happen.

Leon threw up a hand. "Stop, please."

"What? What did I do?"

"You can't move just because you met me. You don't even know if we'll be together in the future."

"Of course we will. We're mates."

Callum wasn't an idiot. It was clear Leon was more hesitant about this than he was, but that was okay. He didn't expect Leon to be as enthusiastic as him or want to throw himself into a relationship immediately. He had no problem with getting to know each other and giving each other space and time to deal with this. He just didn't want it to be too much space, which was why he was already planning his move. Being a freelance graphic designer, he could work from anywhere, but there was only one place where he wanted to be.

He sucked in a breath. "I apologize if I'm overwhelming you. It's kind of what I do, and I haven't been able to change that yet, even though I've tried. I'm not going to move if that's not what you want, but would it be okay if you gave me a way to find you? Because I don't want this to be over before it's even started. I can see you're in shock, and that's perfectly normal, but finding my mate is important to me. I don't want to waste this opportunity."

Leon was still hesitant, so Callum squeaked when he suddenly reached for his hand. Leon hesitated, then squeezed Callum's hand before letting it go again. "Give me your phone number. I'll call you."

Callum narrowed his eyes. "Only if you tell me where you live." He'd heard the people from the van talk about a village, so he was sure he could find it, and he might need to if Leon's hesitation was anything to go by.

Leon sucked in a breath. "I live in Fairview."

There. Had that been as painful as Leon made it sound?

CHAPTER TWO

Leon stared at his phone as if it was going to bite him. As far as he was concerned, it might as well. He'd saved Callum's phone number yesterday, but he had yet to call him, even though he'd promised to.

He just didn't know what to say. Callum was his mate, and Leon should be over the moon happy about meeting him. In a way, he was, but part of his brain couldn't stop pointing out that if he and Callum got together, he'd put Callum in danger.

That wasn't something Leon could do.

It would be better if he stayed away from Callum like he'd stayed away from his family since he'd been released from the lab, but he wasn't sure Callum would let him. Even though Callum didn't have Leon's number, Leon had been stupid yesterday, and he'd told him where he lived. Callum might have trouble finding the village because its location wasn't public knowledge, but eventually, he'd get here, and Leon would have to deal with him when he did.

Wouldn't it be better to do so now? No matter how tempting it was to ignore Callum and focus on the job, the bond would make it impossible, and part of Leon didn't want to ignore his mate anyway. That part of him wanted him to call Callum, get to know him, and eventually build a life with him.

That was the stupid part of Leon—his shifter part.

He glared, but his capybara didn't care. The damn thing just wanted their mate, and it wanted him now. The animal didn't understand that they'd be putting Callum in danger. Leon didn't blame it. He wanted to call Callum, too, but he couldn't ignore the fact that if he did, Callum could get hurt, and that wasn't something he'd be able to live with.

What was he supposed to do?

He doubted that staring at his phone would help him make a decision, but he didn't know what else to do. He wanted someone else to decide for him, but that wasn't possible. No, he needed to be an adult, even though he wasn't sure of any-thing right now. He didn't know how to deal with that. He'd never liked being clueless and lost, and that was how this felt. A big part of him wanted to be done with this problem so he could go on with his life, but Callum wasn't a problem — un-less Leon made him one.

Which was what he was doing.

He groaned and flopped back onto his bed. Unfortunately for him, he'd left his bedroom door open when he'd gone to the bathroom earlier, and Teddy was walking by. He heard him, and before Leon could tell him he was all right, he was already in the bedroom.

"What's going on? What happened?"

Leon couldn't help but smile. Even though he'd left his family behind, he wasn't alone. He'd found his people, and they understood him better than anyone. They'd been through the same hell. They'd been hunted, experimented on, and hurt. Teddy might not have met his mate yet, but he would still understand why Leon was so conflicted.

"Would you leave if I told you I'm fine?" Leon tried.

Teddy looked at him like he was an idiot. "Now I *know* you have a problem. Is it about that guy last night? Tell me, Leon." Teddy paused. "Please."

How could Leon say no? He didn't want to disappoint his friend, and he wanted another perspective on this. He had no doubt that Teddy would see things the way he did, and maybe he could help him let down Callum easily.

There was nothing easy about the situation. Callum wasn't

just a guy. He was Leon's mate, and there would be no letting him down or running from him, even though Leon was trying to convince himself he could.

Leon sucked in a breath. "How do you know it's about him?"

Teddy rolled his eyes. "I know you. I saw the two of you talking, and I'm pretty sure you got his number. Have you called him yet?"

Leon shook his head and looked down at his phone. "I don't know what to say."

"Well, why did you get his number?"

Leon didn't think telling Teddy that it was because he'd felt obligated to would go down well. Besides, it wasn't the entire truth. He *had* felt obligated to get Callum's number, but he'd also wanted it. Without it, he wouldn't be able to reach Callum.

But even though he had Callum's number, he still hadn't called him.

He couldn't help but wonder what Callum was thinking. Was he staring at his phone like Leon? Was he waiting for Leon to make his move and stop being an idiot? Was he already on his way to Fairview, ready to give Leon a piece of his mind?

He didn't know where Leon lived. Leon hadn't given him his address, and he was glad he hadn't. He didn't know Callum at all, but from the little he'd seen yesterday, he wouldn't have been surprised if the man had hunted him down. Something told Leon he'd eventually be able to find him, and he didn't know how to feel about that. Maybe he'd gotten the wrong impression, but something told him Callum was stubborn, especially when he wanted something.

And he'd been clear that he wanted Leon.

He swallowed. He didn't know if he could tell Teddy the entire truth, but he should. It was the only way Teddy would be able to give him good advice, but part of him knew that his friend would slap him on the back of the head if he was honest. Teddy would tell him to stop being an idiot and call Callum to give him a chance because they were mates, and he'd never have this opportunity again.

He wouldn't be wrong.

No matter how much Leon wanted to protect everyone around him, especially the people he cared about, he knew he couldn't. Callum was an adult, and he'd be pissed if Leon took his choice away from him. Leon didn't have a problem doing so when it came to his family, even though he missed them fiercely. His mate was in an entirely different situation, which was why Leon was still here, staring at his phone like an idiot.

"You're starting to worry me," Teddy said. "Is there something else? Maybe more serious?" He sucked in a breath. "Did the guy say or do something to you?"

Leon quickly shook his head because he didn't want Teddy to imagine that anything bad had happened to him, especially when it came to Callum. "He's a nice guy."

"You don't know him, and it's clear he makes you nervous. I can't help you if you don't tell me anything, and something tells me you'd feel better if you were honest." He hesitated. "I promise I won't judge."

Leon leaned forward to kiss Teddy's forehead. "I know. You never do."

Teddy snorted. "I do sometimes. I'm not going to judge you now, though. I just want to know that you're all right."

"I am. I'm conflicted, and I don't know what to do."

"That sounds like a lot for a guy you just met yesterday."

Leon looked down at his hands. "It's not a lot when he's my mate."

For a moment, the silence was absolute. Leon wasn't surprised and gave Teddy time to digest what he just said. He'd had the entire night and barely slept, so he'd had plenty of time. Teddy had just found out.

Teddy made a choking sound and threw himself at Leon. Leon caught him, unsure what had brought on the hug but more than happy to give in. He held Teddy for as long as Teddy needed it, which wasn't long enough, because as soon as he leaned back, he glared at Leon. "I'm so happy for you, but I'm also angry. Why haven't you called him already? Why didn't you invite him to come back with you yesterday? Or maybe you could have gone with him. What the fuck were you thinking?"

"I wasn't thinking. I panicked."

Teddy nodded as if he'd expected that answer. "It makes sense. You didn't expect to meet your mate, and when you did, you didn't know what to do."

Leon nodded—that *was* how he felt. "I still don't know what to do. He's my mate, so, of course, I want to call him, but you know the kind of life we live. Can I really put him in so much danger? Can I pull him into this life without know-ing what will happen to me tomorrow or the day after that?"

Teddy narrowed his eyes. "Look at it from the other side. Can you really lose him? He knows you're mates, right?"

Leon nodded, his stomach churning. "Yeah. We both smelled it."

"Then what do you think he's thinking right now? How do you think he feels? Do you want him to feel like you rejected him? Do you actually want to?"

Those were too many questions. "I just don't want him to be hurt."

"There's nothing that says he will be. Don't be an asshole, Leon. I don't like what you've been doing to your family, but I can understand it. If you do it to your mate, I'll never talk to you again."

That was that. Teddy's threat meant Leon needed to call

Callum because he couldn't lose any of his friends. It was as good a reason to call Callum as any, right?

Callum should have gotten Leon's number yesterday, but he hadn't. Where would he have written it? On his ass?

Leon hadn't called him. If Callum had his phone number, he could have called him himself, but instead, he was left staring at his phone and praying that his mate wouldn't be an asshole and ghost him.

Was that even possible? Could mates stay away from each other? He'd read about it in books and had seen it on TV, but that wasn't real life. Those were romances, and they needed conflict. Sometimes, that conflict happened when one of the mates was an asshole or too stubborn to give in to the bond, but eventually, everything went well. Was that what was happening with Leon? Had he decided to stay away from Callum?

Callum glared at the phone. If Leon thought he'd give in easily, he had another think coming. Callum could be stubborn, even more so when he set his mind to something. He couldn't force Leon to welcome him into his life or even to give him a chance, but that wouldn't stop him from reaching out to him.

Except he didn't have his phone number.

How was he supposed to reach out to Leon when he didn't know how to contact him? Sure, he knew where Leon lived, but that wasn't as helpful as he'd hoped it would be. He'd used his phone to look for Fairview as soon as he got home yesterday, but there hadn't been anything on the map anywhere close to him. He'd stupidly thought Leon lived nearby, but since Leon had arrived with a Nix, he could also live on the other side of the country or even in a different country. Callum didn't think that was likely, but he hadn't realized how much of an idiot he was until he'd understood that he had no way to contact his mate.

He huffed and stuffed another strawberry into his mouth. Had he lost his mate before even getting a chance with him? It sure looked like it, and he didn't know how to feel about it.

Actually, he did. If Leon never called, he'd be destroyed. He'd always thought that his mate would want him, and while he understood that meeting his mate didn't mean everything was right in the world and that they'd fall in each other's arms, he thought he'd at least have a chance to prove to Leon that they could work.

He ate the last strawberry and sighed. Staring at his phone wouldn't help anyone, especially not him. He was too nervous to continue sitting there, which meant he needed to burn some of his nervous energy, and what better way to do so than to fly? This time, though, he'd make sure to take his phone with him. The bag around his neck would be heavy once he was in his bat form, but he could always hang it around Max's neck. He wasn't going to miss Leon's call.

If it ever came.

He got up from his chair and quickly cleaned up the stuff he'd used with his snack, then whistled for Max to come. The dog had no doubt been sleeping on the couch but came running after only a few moments. He looked as eager as Callum felt, so Callum made quick work of leaving his clothes on his porch and putting his phone away. He looped the bag around his neck, then shifted, smiling like an idiot once he was in his bat form. He wasn't sure what that looked like in this form, but he didn't care. He was alone, and no one would see him.

No one but Max.

Callum thought that meeting his mate meant he would be less lonely. He enjoyed living on his own, not having to think about anyone else, and being able to live his life the way he wanted, but sometimes, he wished he had more company.

Max was great, but his conversational skills weren't, and Callum truly had thought that meeting his mate meant he could have all the human company he could ever want. He'd expected not to be annoyed by Leon's presence, but Leon wasn't even here, and Callum was annoyed anyway.

That didn't bode well for their budding relationship.

Of course, Callum doubted there was a budding relationship between them. Leon hadn't even bothered calling him, for fuck's sake. If their roles had been reversed, Callum would have already blown up Leon's phone, trying to get him to answer and convince him to go on a date. He was ready to do pretty much anything to see Leon again, and the thought that he never might made him want to throw up, which was never a pretty thing when he was in his bat form. He needed to keep his fruit inside his stomach, and to do that, he had to stop obsessing over Leon.

Callum spread out his wings, hopped up, and flew.

Max was right behind him. He always was, and Callum reassured himself with the thought that even if Leon wanted nothing to do with him, he'd always have Max. Max was a dog, but it didn't mean Callum didn't love him or that he wasn't precious to him. He was Callum's best friend, as pathetic as that sounded, and Callum wouldn't exchange him for anyone else in the world.

He didn't want to think about how hurt he was over Leon's rejection. He didn't want to think about anything. So, instead, he focused on his wings, on the weight of the phone around his neck, and on how good it felt to be flying.

Eventually, he managed to stop obsessing over Leon and think about nothing but flying, which was why he didn't see the bat coming at him until it was too late.

It wasn't a bat as in the animal like him. No, this one was made of wood, and when it hit him, it sent him flying against a tree. It fucking hurt, and it was a miracle Callum didn't faint.

He was pretty sure one of his wings was broken, and he was already having trouble breathing. Considering the impact, that wasn't a surprise, but it meant he was in trouble.

He tried to fly up, but it was impossible with one of his wings out of commission. He didn't know what was happening but couldn't stay in his bat form, so he shifted.

The pain was blinding. He grabbed his arm, folding it and holding it against his chest since it was almost certainly broken. Thankfully, his phone was still around his neck, and Max had placed himself in front of him. Whoever had wielded that bat wouldn't get to Callum easily.

The man with the bat tried to step around Max, but the dog growled.

"Fucking dog," the man muttered.

"What do you want?" Callum asked as he reached for the bag around his neck.

"Where are they?"

Callum blinked. "Who? I don't know what you're talking about." But he had a sinking feeling that he did. He just didn't want to tell the guy that.

"Don't lie to me. Where are they?"

Callum shook his head. "I don't know." He struggled to get back to his feet. The man tried to step around Max again, but Max wasn't having any of it. He growled and bared his teeth at the man, who jumped back, unwilling to let the dog bite him.

That was all the distraction Callum needed. While the man was focused on Max, Callum turned and ran. He could hear the man shouting, then Max coming after him. As long as Max was there, everything would be all right.

Callum had to believe that.

His arm hurt every time his feet hit the ground, and his ribs were screaming at him to stop, but he ignored all of it and focused on the forest in front of him. Since he couldn't shift, running would be the fastest way to reach safety, but he wasn't sure it would be enough. He hadn't gotten very far from his house, but going there meant taking the asshole back with him. He could lock himself into the house, but that didn't mean the man with the bat wouldn't get inside and hurt him more than he already had.

Callum couldn't go home. He needed to do something else, to save himself, and he didn't know what.

A number flashed in his mind. He wasn't sure it was correct, but he didn't think he had a choice. He needed to at least try, so as he struggled not to drop his phone or hit a tree face-first, he entered the number he'd called yesterday after finding the people in the van and called it.

When Leon's phone rang, it startled him enough that he snatched it up without looking at who was calling. He knew it couldn't be Callum, and he wasn't sure how he felt about that. He still hadn't decided what he wanted to do about his mate, but unfortunately, he didn't think that ignoring him would help.

"Yes?"

"Where are you?" Moore asked.

Leon wasn't sure if he was relieved or not that it was only Moore on the phone. "At home. Are we going on a mission?"

"Not exactly. I got a call from the guy who called us last night, the one who found those people in the van. Someone attacked him, and he's on the run."

Leon shot off his bed, making Teddy squeak in surprise. Leon ignored him, needing to know what was going on. "What happened? Where is he? Is he hurt?"

"I don't know much more than I already told you. Since you talked to him yesterday, you should be able to focus on him and have Teddy shimmer you there. From what he said, there's only one guy after him, so it shouldn't be a problem for you and Teddy to get rid of the attacker and help him."

"We're leaving now."

"Good. Let me know what's going on."

Leon hung up and turned to Teddy. "Callum's been attacked. We have to go."

No one looking at Teddy would think of him as a fighter. He was blond with green eyes and looked gentle. He generally was.

Except when they had to fight. Then, he was ruthless and never hesitated to kill. Leon was glad, because he was going to need that while he tried to avoid freaking out over what was happening to Callum.

They quickly grabbed weapons, and Teddy held out a hand. Leon grabbed it and thought about Callum, about his long dark hair and his dark eyes. He thought about how he wanted to wrap his arms around him and never let him go, about how if Callum ended up being okay, Leon would never let him go.

Teddy shimmered them in the middle of the forest they'd been in the day before, or at least, that was what Leon thought. The forest looked like any forest, full of trees and not much more.

Except for Callum, who was leaning against a tree and breathing hard. He was holding his arm close to his chest, and the position made it clear he was hurt.

"Go to him. I'll find the guy who's after him," Teddy said roughly.

He didn't have to repeat himself. Leon rushed to Callum's side, needing to get his hands on him so he could heal him.

He still didn't understand how his healing ability worked. His hands didn't light up like it happened when a Nix healed. Of course, his healing power didn't work like the healing power of a Nix. He could heal many things, including illnesses like the flu and worse. It took a lot out of him, but he was capable of it, and a broken arm would be nothing to him.

"Callum?" he said as he reached his mate.

Callum jumped and twirled around. The grimace on his face told Leon he was in pain, which was understandable with a broken arm. He raised his hands, hoping Callum would recognize him through the fear.

"Leon?" Callum asked.

"Yeah, it's me. Moore sent me since he saw me talking to you yesterday. Can I take a look at your arm?"

Callum hesitated, then nodded and tried to hold it out. Leon stepped closer, and Max, Callum's dog, growled a little. It caused Leon to stop moving again, but Callum patted his dog's head to reassure him.

"It's all right. Leon is one of the good guys." Callum's gaze flickered at Leon's face. "Or at least, I think so."

"I'm not going to hurt you, if that's what you're asking." Leon supposed he had hurt Callum in a way that wasn't physical by not calling him. That was probably what Callum was referring to, and it made Leon feel guilty.

Now wasn't the moment to think about that, though.

He gently pressed a hand to Callum's arm. Thankfully, Max didn't growl again, so Leon was able to relax. He closed his eyes, focusing on his power.

It was easy to find the break in Callum's arm, but that wasn't the only thing he'd broken. Two of his ribs were cracked, and it had to hurt like hell. He hadn't said anything about it, but he didn't have to. Leon could heal that and so much more, and when it came to his mate, he was ready to use all of his power.

He didn't have to. He'd trained, so he was able to focus on the breaks, and once they were healed, he could focus on the rest. Callum had already started bruising but wouldn't any longer because Leon healed that, too.

As soon as he was done, he opened his eyes and took a step back. Callum stared at him with wide eyes, which wasn't surprising considering what Leon had just done. Most people looked at him that way after he healed them. He wasn't a Nix, so people generally didn't expect him to be able to do that.

"Thank you," Callum said in a shaking voice.

"Can you tell me what happened?"

"Honestly, I'm not sure." He looked around. "I was flying when this guy hit me with a bat." He snickered. "Which shouldn't be funny, but considering I'm a bat shifter, I can't help but find it ironic."

"He hit you with a bat?" Leon didn't find it funny. He found it infuriating and hoped Teddy would bring back the guy who'd done that. Leon needed to have a chat with him.

Callum nodded. "I didn't see it coming. Then I hit a tree, but thankfully, Max was there. As soon as I was back in my human form, he distracted the guy, and I was able to run." He looked around. "I don't know where the guy is. He was behind me."

"Teddy will take care of him."

Callum blinked. "No offense, but he looks like he couldn't hurt a fly."

"Oh, Teddy *wouldn't* hurt a fly. He only hurts people who deserve it, and I'd say that anyone who hits someone with a bat does." Leon wondered if Teddy would leave the guy alive. They might need to interrogate him to understand what he was doing here and why he was attacking bat shifters having fun in the forest.

"The guy kept asking me where *they* are," Callum murmured. "You think he meant the people from the van?"

Leon didn't want to scare Callum. He couldn't lie to him, though. "I'm pretty sure that's what he meant, yes," he agreed. "He has to be a hunter."

Callum shivered, although that might be because he was

naked. Leon was wearing a sweater over his t-shirt, and he quickly took it off and handed it to Callum. Callum stared for a moment before taking it, and Leon was glad to see him putting it on. He needed to take better care of his mate.

Even though he still had no idea what he wanted to do with any of this.

He didn't know what the future would be like, what would end up happening between him and Callum, or anything else, but he was sure of one thing. Every instinct was screaming at him to take care of Callum, and he would. There was no compromising on that. Callum was precious, and that was that.

Leon wasn't that much taller than Callum, but Callum swam in his sweater.

He loved it.

He wrapped the fabric around his naked body, grateful for the warmth and for his mate's scent. It was more soothing than anything Leon could have said, and for a moment, Callum could fool himself into thinking everything was all right. He and his mate had been playing in the forest, and now, it was time for them to go home.

The dream didn't last long. A loud crash came from between the trees, and Callum jumped and moved closer to Leon. Max placed himself in front of both of them, apparently ready to defend Leon now that he'd realized he wasn't a danger. Callum liked that Max felt that way, but he couldn't tell what Leon thought about it or about needing to be here to save Callum.

The blond man who'd been with Leon yesterday — Teddy — appeared. He was dragging the guy who'd hurt Callum, and Callum was surprised when Leon growled and took a step forward.

"That's him?" Leon asked.

Teddy nodded. "Pretty sure it is. He's the only guy I found running through the forest, anyway."

Callum stared in awe as Teddy, who looked so delicate and gentle, threw the bad guy to the ground in front of Callum. The guy didn't appear so strong anymore. Instead, he was shaking and looking from Teddy to Callum, then to Leon. It was clear he didn't know who was more dangerous, and neither did Callum.

The guy tried to run, but Teddy kicked his knee, making him scream. Teddy rolled his eyes, then raised a hand toward Leon. "Let's go home. Moore will want to talk to us and to this guy."

Leon took Teddy's hand, and for a moment, Callum wasn't sure what to do. Teddy grabbed the guy on the ground with his other hand, which meant there was no place for Callum.

They were leaving him behind.

He took a step back, telling himself not to cry in front of his mate. No matter how Leon felt about him, Callum didn't want to show him how vulnerable he was. He didn't want to show him how much he mattered.

But Leon held out his free hand instead of allowing Teddy to shimmer him away. Callum snatched it as if he was afraid Leon would take it away, and he kind of was. He realized he couldn't let Teddy shimmer them away just yet. He was sure he was blushing as he let go of Leon's hand again, then crouched to grab Max. It wasn't the easiest thing to do, since Max was a Labrador, so Callum was thankful for his shifter strength and Leon's healing. He hauled the dog into his arms, then took Leon's hand again.

It was clear Teddy was doing his best not to smile, but he wasn't great at it. His lips kept twitching, and when Callum turned to him, he beamed.

Then they were gone.

Callum had used Nix apps several times over the years, so

he knew what shimmering felt like. His stomach churned, like always, but they arrived before he could feel sick. He looked around, curious to find out more about Fairview. That was where they had to be, right? Teddy had said they needed to go home, and yesterday, Leon told Callum that Fairview was home.

"Why don't you take Callum home?" Teddy told Leon. "You can check him over again, and I'm sure he'd be grateful for a shower and clothes."

Callum didn't want to go home but wasn't about to beg. "I can take care of myself," he said.

Teddy winked. "I'm sure you can, but you should let your mate take care of you."

Callum blinked, trying to make sense of what Teddy was saying. Leon had told him he and Callum were mates. That had to mean something, right?

"I'll drag this guy to the cell," Teddy continued, turning to Leon. "Moore will want to know we're back, and I'm sure he'll be interested in talking to this asshole."

The asshole whimpered and tried to pull away, but Teddy gave him a good shake.

Callum loved him. He loved how strong Teddy was and how he wasn't ashamed of it or of what he could do. He wanted to be Teddy when he grew up.

"Come on," Leon murmured as he cupped Callum's elbow and steered him away from Teddy. "I'll take you to my room. I can check you over again, and you can take a shower."

"You're taking me to your home?"

"Where did you think I was taking you?"

Callum followed his mate with Max on their heels. He didn't know how to answer Leon's question. "To *my* home."

"Yet you were so eager to move here yesterday when we talked."

"I'm still eager to move. I just didn't feel you were."

Leon stumbled, then quickly caught himself. "We just met."

"Which is why I didn't come with you yesterday. I knew it would be too much."

Thankfully, Leon appeared to be relaxed. It was clear he was also freaking out, but as long as he wasn't running away screaming, Callum could work with it.

He had to. He wasn't giving up Leon as long as Leon didn't clearly tell him he wanted nothing to do with him. Callum didn't think that was the case. He understood why Leon was freaking out and even why he hadn't called him. Neither of them had expected to meet their mate yesterday, but they had and had to deal with it the best way they could. The situation wouldn't be the same for both of them, and it was something Callum could understand. If Leon needed time and space, Callum would be happy to give them to him.

But he wanted Leon to communicate and tell him that. He wanted Leon to be honest, even if it was only to tell Callum that he was freaking out and didn't know what to do.

Callum felt the same way.

He didn't want to push Leon into anything he wasn't ready for, but he still wanted to be close to him and feel safe. Something told him that he would if he moved to Fairview, especially if the guy who'd attacked him was involved with what had happened yesterday. He'd clearly known where to find Callum, so who was to say someone else wouldn't come? Maybe next time, Callum wouldn't be as lucky as he had been today. Maybe next time, he'd be seriously hurt and unable to run, and these guys would get what they wanted.

Callum wasn't sure what that was. Maybe it had only been information, or maybe the guy had been convinced Callum was hiding the people from the van. Callum didn't think he'd have survived their encounter either way. He was scared to go home, not only for himself but also for Max. His dog would react to protect him if he had to, and he might get hurt because of that. Callum couldn't lose him.

He hoped that eventually Leon would get over the hang-ups he had about their bond and want him, but he wasn't in a hurry. Maybe it would be a good idea to woo Leon. Maybe Callum could make him feel strongly enough about him that Leon wouldn't want to leave once this mess was over.

But first, he had to tell Leon he was moving to Fairview. "I'm not going home," he declared.

Leon didn't seem surprised. "I didn't think you were. It's too dangerous."

Callum was glad they agreed on that. "You think someone else will try to find me?"

"I wouldn't be surprised. This guy clearly thought you knew where the people from the van are. I don't think they'll stop until they get them back, and if that means hurting you, they won't hesitate. They're ruthless and cruel."

"You talk like you know who they are and have met them before."

Leon's expression was grim. "I have, and I don't want you to encounter them ever again. So maybe it *is* a good idea for you to move here."

Callum pressed his lips together so he wouldn't beam like an idiot. "I feel the same way."

"Of course you would." Leon looked at Callum with a knowing glance. "That's what you've been angling for since yesterday."

"Can you blame me? My mate is here."

To Callum's surprise, Leon didn't ditch him to run away. Instead, he stared at Callum for a moment before nodding. "I'll keep you safe," he promised.

Callum told himself he wasn't going to cry, even though his eyes prickled. "I know."

He did. No matter how Leon felt about their bond, he was

a protector, and Callum needed protection. Leon would give it to him.

CHAPTER THREE

Callum had been staying in Fairview for a few days now, but Leon didn't know if it was a good thing. Anyone else would have said yes, but he couldn't.

He scowled at the fruit in front of him. He'd had an idea as he walked into the grocery store, but now, he wondered if it was stupid. He was confused, and he didn't know how to un-confuse himself.

The problem was entirely his. He wanted Callum to be in Fairview so he could make sure his mate was safe, but at the same time, every time Callum wasn't in his sight, he started panicking. It didn't matter that he knew Callum would be fine here. Now that the hunters had gone after him, Leon couldn't stop thinking about what would have happened if they'd caught him. As it was, that hunter had hurt his mate, broken his arm, and cracked several of his ribs, and Leon was pissed. Even more so, he was terrified that something else would happen to Callum.

He didn't know how to deal with any of this. He'd stayed away from his family because he didn't want them to be involved with the hunters or the labs, and even though he missed them fiercely, he didn't regret his decision. Knowing they were safe was more important than seeing them, although he was sure they wouldn't feel the same way if he reached out to them. For now, he had no plans of doing so. The hunters and the labs were still a danger, and he and the other mutants weren't done fighting them yet.

Which was why he was panicky over Callum. Callum

wasn't on the other side of the country, safe and not knowing what happened to Leon. He was right there, had seen what the hunters did, and was too vulnerable. Even in his bat form, he wasn't a fighter. He didn't have fangs and claws, which meant that if someone caught him, he'd be in trouble. It was Leon's job to ensure he wasn't, but besides locking him in his house and telling him he could never leave, Leon wasn't sure how to do it. He didn't know Callum well, but something told him his mate wouldn't be happy with that solution.

Where did that leave Leon? He realized that all of these feelings were his problem and no one else's. They were due to what he'd lived through and what he'd seen since then, and he needed to learn to let go. It wasn't easy, especially since he didn't know what he wanted yet.

Of course he wanted Callum, but his fears made him hesitate. At the same time, he didn't want to push Callum away so much that he'd lose him. He was stuck between wanting more and needing less, and it was fucking confusing.

Maybe he could take small steps. Callum knew what he did for a living and what the hunters did, and he hadn't run away. He was settling down in Fairview, making friends, and behaving like he'd always lived here. Leon was pretty sure that Callum wanted them to be together, but he hadn't pushed or demanded anything. He texted Leon every day, which was enough to put a smile on Leon's face, but he didn't try to force him into seeing each other or anything like that. He could tell that Leon was hesitant, and he didn't seem to mind.

But Leon did. Part of him yearned for his mate, even though pulling him deeper into his world would be dangerous. But Callum was already in his world, and he'd already been hurt. Would it be so bad if they took another step in their relationship? Leon had been avoiding Callum, but he was tired.

He wanted this for himself. The lab and what the scientists

had done to him had taken a lot from him. He'd lost the life he had before, his family, and the people he loved. He'd found a new place to live and more people to care about, but it wasn't the same, and he didn't know if it ever would be. He needed to rebuild what the hunters and the labs had destroyed, and maybe he could start with Callum.

He grabbed a melon and added it to his cart. He'd seen Callum eat fruit several times, so he knew how much of it his mate could put away. The melon wouldn't be enough.

Next, he reached for the strawberries. He wasn't really into apples and pears, but he suspected Callum would appreciate them, so he grabbed a few of both. That should be enough for today, right? Leon had a plan and didn't want to be carting fruit all over town.

Once he had what he wanted, he headed to the pet food aisle. There, he grabbed some treats for Max, since where Callum went, Max followed. Leon couldn't say he was sorry about it. The dog had saved Callum's life when the hunter had attacked, and if it was up to Leon, he'd buy him a steak rather than dog treats. He doubted Callum would appreciate it, which was why he restrained himself.

He'd always been a cat person but had a new respect for dogs.

He paid and left the grocery store once he had everything he thought he'd need. Callum had been staying in one of the empty houses in the village. Leon had wondered why there were so many of them, so he'd asked Hayes, certain he would know since he was Rikar's mate. The answer had surprised him, yet at the same time, it hadn't.

When Rikar had become the leader of the tribe and they'd started rescuing people from the labs, he'd decided to build more houses than they needed. Some of the people they'd rescued had decided they didn't want to go back to the life they'd lost, and it had been easier for them to stay with the tribe. That meant the tribe needed more space, so they'd built more houses and became a little town.

It had come in handy when the mutants had moved there, but even with them, there were still empty houses waiting to be lived in, and Callum had moved into one of them.

Permanently.

Before choosing the house, he'd asked Leon his opinion of the houses. Leon wasn't an idiot, and he knew Callum had done so because he expected Leon to move in with him eventually. It had touched him that while he was working so hard to keep distance between them, Callum was already thinking about the future they'd share. He was showing Leon he cared without pushing, seemingly realizing that it was the only way Leon would give him a chance.

Well, Leon was ready to do so.

He reached Callum's door, but he didn't knock right away. The grocery store bags were heavy, so he set them down and sucked in a breath. He could do this. It was only some fruit and dog treats. He didn't expect anything in exchange, and Callum wouldn't see it as anything more than it was.

An opening to Leon's heart.

Leon knocked before he could chicken out. He didn't understand why the thought of seeing his mate made him so nervous, but he needed to get over it and all the other negative feelings he had when it came to Callum. Some people believed that mates met when they most needed each other, and Callum clearly had needed him when they'd met. Maybe the same went for him. Maybe he needed Callum to get out of the funk he was in and stop fearing that something would happen to the people he cared about.

When Callum didn't answer, Leon knocked again. The door stayed closed, and he couldn't hear any noise inside the house, not even Max. He told himself that Callum was probably all right, but he could feel panic tightening his chest. He needed to find his mate. What if something had happened to Callum? What if he was hurt and needed him?

Leon walked around the house, peeking through the windows, but as he'd expected, the house was empty.

His mate was gone.

What was Leon supposed to do? It was possible that Callum was in the forest, but there would be no way for him to find his mate. Besides, there were no clothes on the back porch or anything else that would indicate that Callum had shifted. He was just gone, and no matter how many times Leon told himself everything would be right, he wasn't sure he could believe it.

"I'm telling you, there's no better movie," Teddy said as he pointed the fry he was eating at Hayes. "It's a classic."

Hayes wrinkled his nose. "Yeah, but there's a mummy. I don't want to watch that."

"There's also Brendan Fraser. Who wouldn't want to watch a movie with him? And he's only the tip of the iceberg. That movie is how I realized I was pansexual."

Hayes didn't look convinced, and Callum almost laughed. He knew what Teddy was talking about, and while he could appreciate how beautiful the women in that movie were, he was still decidedly gay. He wouldn't mind re-watching it, though. He always had time for that.

But his mind had been preoccupied lately, and it still was. On paper, it shouldn't be. Teddy had helped him pack up his house and move, and since he'd been renting, he wouldn't have to worry about selling or anything like that. He hadn't owned much, but everything fit into his new home.

A home he'd chosen with Leon.

Callum hadn't asked him to move in yet, and he wasn't planning to anytime soon. He'd wanted Leon's input in choosing the house because eventually, it would be Leon's home, too, but he hadn't mentioned that. He was sure Leon knew, anyway, but as long as neither of them said it out loud, Callum supposed Leon could ignore it.

Just like he was ignoring a bunch of things he probably shouldn't.

Callum sighed. He understood where Leon was coming from and kept telling himself not to be impatient, but it wasn't always easy. He'd met his mate, and he should be happy. They should be planning their future, spending time together, and building a life, but instead, Leon kept a distance between them that Callum wasn't sure how to cross.

Part of the problem was that he didn't know Leon well, which was one of the reasons he was here with Teddy and Hayes today. When Teddy had invited him out for lunch, he'd jumped on the opportunity, and not just because he wanted to find out more about his mate. The village was his new home, and Teddy and Hayes were Leon's friends. More than that, they were his family, and Callum hoped they would eventually become his. They knew Leon much better than he did, and maybe by the end of the meal, he'd be able to ask them about his mate without feeling like he was using them.

So far, their lunch had gone great. They'd talked about movies, and Hayes had declared he'd never seen *The Mummy* after Teddy had mentioned he'd re-watched it last night. Clearly, Teddy considered that a crime, and he was already planning a watch party.

"You're coming, right?" he asked Callum.

Callum grinned. "I wouldn't miss it for anything." He hesitated. "Will Leon be there?"

"If he knows what's good for him," Teddy grumbled. "He's still avoiding you?"

"I think that more than avoiding me, he's freaking out. To be honest, I am, too."

"Why? Has something happened, or are you still trying to wrap your minds around the fact that you're mates?" Hayes asked, leaning forward.

Callum took a moment to answer. He didn't want Leon's best friends to worry, but it was clearly too late. "I'm happy about having met Leon. It's good to know that I have fulfilled that dream and can start thinking about the future. The problem is him, and I'm not sure how to deal with it. It's almost like he wants to stay away from me, yet when he doesn't know where I am, he freaks out and needs to protect me."

It was too much and not enough, but more importantly, Callum didn't want Leon to freak out every time he was out of his sight for the rest of their lives. Callum understood the reason behind it, and he couldn't even say Leon was wrong. After all, the first time after they'd met that he'd been alone, he'd been attacked.

But he didn't want Leon to treat him as if he was fragile. He didn't want Leon to be his shadow. Even today, after Teddy and Hayes had invited him to the diner, he'd known that if he texted Leon to tell him about it, he'd come to find them. It wasn't that Callum didn't want Leon here. In fact, he would have loved it if his mate had been eating lunch with them.

But not because Leon thought Callum would be attacked if he wasn't with him.

Callum tried to explain all of that to Teddy and Hayes, but it was hard to put into words. That didn't seem to be a problem, because Teddy was nodding, which was a relief. He and Hayes would be able to give him good advice.

"Well, it makes sense that he's frightened for you," Hayes pointed out. "You were attacked and hurt. He healed you, but I think anyone would have freaked out if their mate had been beaten up with a baseball bat."

Callum wrinkled his nose. "I wasn't beaten up. It was just

one hit, and I only broke my arm."

"And cracked two ribs. Plus, you were bruised."

"Leon talked to you." Of course he had. Why wouldn't he talk about his mate with his best friends?

"You need to talk to him," Teddy declared. "What happened to us in the labs left scars. We don't deal with it the same way, but you're not the first to notice that Leon panics when he can't see the people he cares about. Initially, it wasn't easy for him since we regularly go on raids, but he adapted, and I'm sure he can do the same with you."

"How did he accept that the three of you wouldn't spend the rest of your lives attached at the hip?"

"He saw we could defend ourselves," Teddy said with a grin. "Maybe that's what you should do. I'd really talk to him if I were you, though. He needs to know he's making you uncomfortable."

"I wouldn't call it uncomfortable," Callum said, wriggling in his seat.

"That's bullshit, but fine. I get why you don't want to broach the subject, and I don't want to, either. Leon can't lock you up, though. You need to live your life, and that includes leaving your home, going out for lunch and to the grocery store, things like that. You have to be able to live your life because if you can't, you'll turn bitter."

And if he did, he might come to blame Leon for everything.

He hadn't had much of a life before. He'd always been a loner, and most of the time, Max was enough company. Even now, he was under the table, snuggled on Callum's feet, snoring a little. For the longest time, it had been only the two of them, and in many ways, it still was.

But Callum hoped that, eventually, it would be the three of them. He wanted a future with Leon, so he needed to be honest with him about his needs.

A woman walked past their table. Callum didn't think

much of it until she stopped and stared at him. Teddy and Hayes seemed amused, so Callum wasn't worried, but he still wondered what the woman wanted.

"This is Olga," Teddy explained. "She's Moore's second in command."

So she was a mutant. Callum eyed her, wondering what kind of ability she had. He wasn't going to ask, because it would be rude, but maybe once she was gone, Teddy and Hayes would tell him. He was fascinated by the fact that a lot of the people around him could do things he could only ever dream about. He was even a bit jealous, although he'd never want to go through what they'd gone through.

Olga beamed. "I wouldn't worry too much if I were you. Everything will be all right in the end."

She turned and continued walking, joining an older woman sitting at a table nearby. Callum stared, not knowing what to think about what she'd said. "What did she mean?"

Teddy patted Callum's hand. "She sees the future. If she says everything will be all right, then everything will be all right."

Callum wasn't sure he believed in anyone knowing the future, but what did he know? He was just now wrapping his mind around what the mutants could do, and knowing the future seemed possible, even though it was outlandish.

Besides, he *wanted* to believe Olga.

Leon told himself not to freak out right away and took time to explore part of the forest around the house. He'd known he wouldn't find Callum there, though. Something told him Callum was nowhere near him, and in the end, he couldn't stop himself.

He called Moore.

He wasn't sure what he thought his leader could do about

the situation, but hearing his voice was enough to calm him down. It didn't stop him from freaking out entirely, but at least he felt like he could breathe.

"What's going on?" Moore asked.

"I can't find Callum anywhere. He's not home or in the forest close by."

There was a pause as if Moore was thinking about what Callum had said. "You're freaking out about this?"

He knew Leon too well. "Yeah. I know I shouldn't, but I can't stop my mind from going there. What if he's hurt and needs me? What if the hunters found him and took him away?"

"And what if he's in town having lunch with two of your friends?"

Leon blinked. His legs felt like jelly at the relief of hearing that Callum was all right, and he quickly sat on the porch steps. "He is?"

"Yeah. I just got a text from Olga. I didn't understand why she was telling me about it, but now I do."

She'd known that Leon was panicking and that he'd call Moore. Leon was never sure how he felt about her ability, but he couldn't deny that sometimes, it came in handy.

"Breathe," Moore ordered.

Leon closed his eyes and did his best to obey. It was enough to know that Callum was safe and protected for him to stop obsessing over the possibility that he was hurt, and once he did, he realized how ridiculous he'd been.

"I'm sorry about this," he murmured.

"I'm not. I want you to rely on me and the others if you need us. We're family, right?"

"Right," Leon confirmed.

He might not have his biological family anymore, but he'd found a second family, and all of them were well-trained and had abilities that meant they could defend themselves. Even so, it had been hard not to stay with them constantly when they went on raids. He'd had to work hard on not panicking every time he couldn't see Teddy and Hayes, but he'd managed, and his life was better for it.

It looked like he'd have to do the same kind of work when it came to Callum. He didn't want to suffocate his mate with his presence and attention, but he didn't think it would be as easy as it had been with Teddy and Hayes, and that had been hell. Callum wasn't just one of his best friends. He was his mate, and the thought of something happening to him made Leon's mouth go dry.

"We need to talk about this," Moore said gently. "I understand why you were scared, but you have to loosen up and give Callum space to live his life. He's only been here for a few days, and I swear I haven't seen him alone around town yet. Every time he's not home, you're with him, and I'm afraid you're going to push him in the wrong direction if you continue. This is a new place for him with many new people. He needs to find his place in Fairview, and he won't be able to if you shadow him all the time. Besides, it's not only that. Mates need time apart and to trust each other."

"I trust him," Leon quickly said.

"You don't trust that he can protect himself."

"Can you blame me? He was hurt just a few days ago."

"He was," Moore agreed. "And I was hurt a few weeks ago on that raid."

"That's different."

"How is it different? I was hurt, you healed me, and I'm fine. I'm not planning to take Callum on a raid. He's in Fairview, which means he's safe and that you shouldn't worry so much about him. The hunters can't find him here, and if they can't find him, they can't hurt him."

That much was true. The village was a secret, and even though people in the paranormal community knew about it, most didn't know where it was. They just knew it was a place where the survivors of the labs lived and where the people who had rescued them kept them safe. No one moved here unless Rikar approved it, and since that meant he'd approved everyone, Leon really should feel that Callum was safe.

"Logically, I know he's safe and that I don't need to stick with him every second of every day," he explained. "But no matter how hard I try, I can't stop imagining everything that might happen to him anyway. What if he leaves the village?"

"Why should he?"

"I don't know." Leon was frustrated with himself. "I already lost so much. We all did, in one way or another. I don't want to lose him, too."

"You might lose him if you don't give him space, though. That would be the same result, but it would happen in a different way. Is it something you can deal with?"

He was right. Leon needed to get a grip, and while it wasn't easy, Callum was worth working and fighting for. Leon was safe here, and he'd never go back to the labs. Leon would make sure of that. But he didn't have to keep an eye on Callum all the time to make sure that didn't happen. His mate was safe in the village, and the people Leon cared the most about were keeping an eye on him. Knowing that Callum was with Teddy and Hayes made it easier for Leon to breathe. He wasn't the only one who could protect Callum if anything happened. In fact, a lot of the people who lived in the village knew how to fight and would defend anyone being hurt. *That* was what Leon had to keep in mind.

That, and the knowledge that he might lose Callum if he didn't step back. He wouldn't be able to blame the hunters or the labs if that happened. He'd only have himself to blame, and frankly, he didn't know how he'd survive if he didn't have Callum.

They weren't together, but the possibility was there. The

only reason there was some distance between them was that Leon had put it there. It had felt safest for his heart to keep his mate at arm's length because if he was already panicky at the thought of not seeing him now, how much worse would it be if they were bonded?

Maybe Leon was going about this in the wrong way. He didn't want to lose Callum, not because of the hunters, and not at his own hands. Something needed to change before he pushed Callum too far, and that something was him.

"Thanks for this," he told Moore.

"I'm sure you were already aware of all of this. You just needed to be reminded of it." He hesitated. "I understand where you're coming from. It's never easy to let your guard down, especially when you know how much evil is out there, but you need to be able to do so. We all deserve our happy ending. We went through hell, and I think finding our mate is one way for Fate to apologize. Don't mess things up with Callum. You'll regret it, and you'll both be unhappy. I'm not saying that you need to stop being yourself, but try to relax and, more importantly, give Callum space to be himself and create his new future."

Leon needed to do the same. He hadn't expected to meet his mate, but he had, and his life had changed because of that. It was down to him whether his life would change for the better or worse, and he knew what he wanted.

He just had to pray he'd be strong enough to do what needed to be done to get it.

Callum was focused on his conversation with Teddy and Hayes when the diner door opened. He glanced up, not expecting it to be anyone he knew, but Leon came in through the door.

Callum stopped talking. He stared at his mate, wondering

why he was there. Was it to tell him that he should have called before leaving the house? Did he want to reassure himself that Callum was all right? Callum tried to understand Leon's feelings, but he couldn't without a complete bond. Leon's expression was serene, but considering what Callum knew of Leon, there was no way he felt that way.

When Leon reached their table, Callum held his breath, not knowing what to expect. It wasn't Leon smiling at them as if this were a perfectly normal situation.

"I see the three of you were having lunch without me," he said.

"There's a reason we didn't call you," Teddy pointed out. "We wanted to get to know your mate without you around."

For a second, Leon's expression fell. He quickly schooled it. "You hurt me, Teddy. I thought you were one of my best friends."

Teddy looked like he wasn't sure what to make of Leon's words. Callum didn't.

He got to his feet. "Hey, we were just about done. Do you want to sit with us, or should I leave with you?"

"We can stay a while longer if you want. I want you to have friends."

That was *definitely* not what Callum had expected. "That's great, but I'm sure Teddy and Hayes have better things to do." He looked at them and tried to convey the fact that he wanted to go with Leon, but he wasn't sure he'd managed until Teddy grinned.

"Go. We invited you, so we'll pay for your meal. If you have any trouble with that thing we talked about, call me, all right?"

That *thing* that Callum could have problems with was Leon, and while Callum was puzzled by Leon's behavior, he didn't think he'd have a problem with him. Leon would never hurt him. He just wanted to make sure Callum was safe, and

Callum could understand that. He wanted to make sure Leon was safe, too. He just wasn't as frantic about it.

It made sense. Callum's life had been normal. On the other hand, Leon had been taken from his family and his life, tortured and changed, and eventually freed. The fact that he wasn't in the lab anymore didn't change what he'd experienced there, including the pain and horror he'd seen and lived through. Callum knew Leon had never contacted his family, even after being freed, and he could understand why. Leon's life was dangerous, especially for someone who couldn't defend themselves.

The description fit Callum to a T, but it wouldn't stop him. He was willing to do pretty much anything to be part of Leon's life. If he had to take self-defense classes, he would. If he had to spend the rest of his life in Fairview, he was pretty sure it wouldn't be a hardship. He was a loner, anyway, and from what he'd seen, the town was pretty much perfect.

It was small, but it had everything someone might need. He'd never have to go far to get food or anything else, and he didn't want to. His dream had always been to settle in a small town, and Fairview was great.

Especially because Leon lived here, too.

It didn't matter if it took Leon years to get over his fear that Callum was in danger. They'd get over it, and in the meantime, they'd learn to live with it.

Callum said goodbye to Hayes and Teddy and followed Leon out of the diner. Max trotted at his feet, probably happy to get some fresh air. Callum kept the leash short and walked along with Leon down the sidewalk.

"I went to your house," Leon said, as he headed back that way.

Callum wasn't surprised to see that was where Leon was headed, and he didn't mind. He wanted them to have some time together and to get to know each other beyond the fear and the mess of the situation they'd been in when they'd met. There was no better place for that to happen than Callum's home. It was private, and eventually, they'd both live there.

He couldn't wait.

"Sorry I wasn't there," he told Leon. "Teddy and Hayes came knocking an hour ago. I didn't expect them to invite me out for lunch."

"It's fine. You didn't do anything wrong, and you should have lunch with friends if that's what you want."

Callum wasn't quite sure who this Leon was. "How did you feel when you realized I wasn't home and that you didn't know where to find me?"

Leon hesitated, then huffed. "I want to deny that I panicked, but I can't, because that's what I did. I searched the forest around the house, and then I called Moore."

"What did he say?"

"Olga had texted him to let him know you were with Hayes and Teddy. He also said that I needed to get over my fear that something will happen to you if I don't have you in my sight twenty-four seven, and he's right. I don't want to push you away."

Callum was touched and hopeful. "You're not pushing me away."

"Maybe not now, but eventually, you'll have enough of my behavior." He looked around, but they were already on Callum's street, and it was empty except for them. That was another thing Callum loved about Fairview. He could walk everywhere and be home in under five minutes, whatever he did in town.

"I know that this is a hang-up I'll have to deal with eventually, and I'm trying. The problem is that I saw so many horrible things. Now that I have you, the most precious person I can ever have in my life, I'm terrified at the thought of something happening to you. I can't stop thinking about what will happen if the hunters find you. They'd take you to one of the labs, and I know what would be done to you there."

Callum's heart broke for Leon. He wasn't sure he could help his mate through this, but he didn't know if Leon would be willing to allow anyone else to do so. What he did with the mutants was still very much a secret, and they couldn't be open about it to most people, not even other shifters. Callum wasn't equipped to deal with Leon's fears, and he wasn't sure Leon was, either, but there had to be someone out there who could help.

For now, though, he needed to focus on his mate. "I might not have details about what happened to you in the lab, but I have a good imagination. I don't blame you for freaking out about it when it comes to me."

Leon smiled. "I'm doing my best to stop feeling that way, but I can't make any promises. It won't happen quickly."

Callum took his hand. "I don't need it to happen quickly. I just need you to work on it and give me a chance. If it makes you feel better, I promise to text you when I leave the house. I'm not saying I'll stop going out on my own, but at least that way, you'll know where I am. I also promise not to leave Fairview alone."

Some people would have felt restricted, but Callum didn't. He was doing this for their bond and their future, and if this was what it took to make Leon feel better about their relationship and to help him deal with his fears, then Callum would do it.

Leon was his future as much as he was Leon's future. They needed to find a way to make it work, which meant they both had to compromise. There was no doubt that Leon was the one with the most hang-ups between the two of them, but that didn't matter. The only thing that did was that they were both willing to do anything to be together.

"I don't know what I did to deserve you as a mate, but I'll

always be thankful," Leon murmured.

"You were you. That's all you needed to deserve a mate like me." To make sure Leon understood he wasn't kidding, Callum kissed him.

It was their first kiss, and maybe it would have been better not to do it in the middle of the street, but they were alone, and Callum couldn't resist anymore. He wanted Leon to understand that he wasn't going anywhere and that he was willing to work hard for their future together.

Leon's lips were soft, and he instantly gave in to Callum's demands. He opened his mouth, and Callum slipped his tongue in and sighed, finally tasting his mate. It wasn't the kind of taste that would bond them, but it was perfect anyway.

This was Callum's future. *Leon* was Callum's future.

Callum wouldn't have it any other way, no matter how many difficulties they'd have to face.

CHAPTER FOUR

Leon hadn't scared just Callum the other day. The panic he'd felt had scared him, too, and he didn't like it. He didn't want to live the rest of his life in fear.

The problem was that he didn't know how to get rid of that fear and of thinking that something would happen to Callum if he wasn't with him.

He thought about it while he picked up more fruit at the grocery store. Callum really enjoyed his fruit, and Leon was happy to indulge him. The look on Callum's face when Leon cared for him like this was priceless, and Leon would do anything to see it again.

Hence the need for more fruit.

Leon felt like they were finally moving forward. The only reason they hadn't done so sooner was him, and while he still wasn't there yet, he'd finally realized that he wanted Callum. Why else would he be so terrified that something would happen to him? The only reason he could think of was that he cared about him, and he liked that he did. He could do without the fear, but he suspected that once he was over that, he'd really love the life they'd share.

But he needed to find a way to make it happen, and that way wasn't to freak out every time Callum was out by himself. It was why Leon was resisting the urge to grab his phone and text Callum. He didn't know where his mate was, and while being aware of that made his mouth taste like ash, he was proud of himself for not rushing to Callum's house. He'd go there slowly once he was done with his grocery shopping.

But he had to find a way to deal with this fear. Callum had suggested talking to a professional, and for the first time, Leon was ready to consider that option. But he'd have to do more than just that. Talking to someone would help, but it would take too long. Leon wanted to give Callum what he wanted now, but how was he supposed to do it?

Maybe getting rid of the reason he was so afraid would help. He didn't think he could kill all the hunters, but he could certainly try. That was what the mutant group had been created to do. They existed to free the people in the labs and avenge the ones who hadn't made it. Sometimes, the anger Leon felt at the thought of all these people was scary but not scarier than the thought of losing Callum.

But he couldn't do so now. He had to focus on Callum, so after paying for the fruit, he headed to Callum's house. He thought about what had happened the last time he'd done this, but he tried not to freak out too much. He was a work in progress, so it wasn't a surprise that part of him was petrified, but he still managed to get to Callum's house and knock on his front door instead of running there and barging in.

This time, it opened.

Leon breathed out in relief and smiled at Callum. Callum smiled back, his expression telling Leon he was puzzled.

"Hey. Were we supposed to meet?" Callum asked. He was holding Max's collar so the dog wouldn't sneak out.

Leon shook his head and raised his bag. "No, but I thought I would surprise you with some fruit."

The look on Callum's face was adorable. His eyes lit up, and he quickly let Leon in, making grabby hands at the bag.

"What did you buy?"

"A little bit of everything. I still don't know what your favorite fruit is." And Leon didn't like that. He'd allowed his fears to take over, which meant that he and Callum hadn't gotten to know each other well yet. They could fix that, thankfully.

They could fix a lot of things if they tried.

Callum took the bag to the kitchen. "I don't have a favorite fruit. I love all fruit."

"That's not possible. No one loves every aspect of a thing."

"I'm not lying. I haven't yet found a fruit I don't like."

Callum started emptying the bag, and Leon sat at the counter to watch him. Max sat at his feet, so Leon stroked his head.

Callum was a delight. Leon didn't have the same love for fruit, but watching Callum was enough. *That* was what he loved about this situation.

He didn't love Callum yet, but how long would that take? If they continued spending time together, not long at all, and while Leon might have been afraid of that once, he wasn't anymore. So what if he fell in love with his mate? He wanted to spend the rest of his life with him. He might as well start right away.

If Callum had been anyone else, Leon would have been freaking out at his thoughts, but Callum was Callum. He was Leon's mate, and that meant everything. Leon hadn't understood how true that was before, but he did now.

He hadn't known what to do with Callum before, and he still wasn't a hundred percent sure, but he didn't *have* to know. He just had to be himself, get over his absurd fear, and find a way to make things work. Callum had given Leon a lot of slack, space, and time to figure his shit out, and it was time to actually do it instead of letting fear guide every step of his life.

He needed to start somewhere. As he watched Callum gleefully cut into a melon, he knew he had to explain why he was the way he was. Callum had the bare bones of the story, but Leon had avoided talking about it in detail. There was nothing he wanted less, but considering who Callum was and their situation, Leon felt he deserved to know. It would be easier to be honest while Callum was focused on something else, although Leon wasn't sure how long things would stay that way. Still, now felt like the best moment to do this.

He cleared his throat. "Before the hunters captured me, I had a family," he started. "My parents and my brother. I thought things would stay that way forever and had no reason to think otherwise. Then I was taken."

Callum put down his knife. "You don't have to talk about this."

"I know you would never demand to know about it, but that's why I want to tell you. I want you to understand why I behave the way I do. I know it's overwhelming and a lot to deal with, and you never signed up for this. You didn't choose to be my mate, but you are, and I want to make things as easy on you as I can."

"You don't have to make things easy on me. Relationships aren't easy, and I didn't expect this one to be."

"Even though I'm your mate?"

Callum snorted, stuffed a bit of melon into his mouth, and began chewing it.

Leon thought he'd never seen anyone so beautiful. Callum knew what he wanted in life. He hadn't hesitated to move to Fairview after they'd met, even though there was no way for him to know how things would go between them. He wanted Leon, and he was working toward that goal. He hadn't let anything stop him, not even fear. Leon wished he could be as brave as his mate, and while he wasn't sure he ever could be, he could try. That was what he was attempting to do right now.

"I expected our relationship to be complicated because we're mates," Callum said. "That's how it works, isn't it? Mates are in it forever, but the fact that they're destined to be together and spend the rest of their lives as a couple makes everything more complicated. You can't leave when something goes wrong, or it gets hard. We have to face things together and work as a unit, and many people don't have that in them."

"You do."

Callum nodded. "I think I do, anyway. I'm not giving up on you or on us, Leon. It doesn't matter that you're scared and don't know what you're doing. To be honest, I don't know what I'm doing, either. That's not going to stop me from trying to make you happy. I'm going to try until I get it right."

There was no fear left in Leon. He wanted what Callum was describing. He wanted his mate to make him happy, and he wanted to make his mate happy. He might not know how to do it, but eventually, he'd find out. In the meantime, he and Callum could work things out together.

That was how things were meant to be.

Callum was surprised when Leon started talking about his time in the lab. If Leon wanted to tell him about it, he'd listen, but he couldn't say he was eager to learn more details. What little he'd gotten from Teddy and Hayes and seeing how traumatized Leon was had been enough for him and his imagination to come up with a scenario. He didn't *want* more details, and he wasn't going to push Leon into giving them to him.

The thought of what his mate had gone through in that lab made him want to throw up. He couldn't understand how a human being could hurt another human the way those scientists had, although maybe that was the problem. Maybe those people didn't see shifters like human beings, and that was why they treated them like that. Still, as far as Callum was concerned, it made them monsters. Even if they didn't consider shifters human beings but rather animals, they were still experimenting on animals, and that wasn't something Callum could accept.

His stomach churned, and he mournfully eyed the melon. He wanted to continue eating but wasn't sure his stomach could take this kind of conversation. Still, if Leon needed this, Callum wanted to give it to him. It was the first time Leon had opened up to him like this, and he didn't want to ruin the moment.

"I just want you to understand why I freak out so badly when I don't know where you are," Leon said slowly.

"I think I know. You've told me a bit, and I talked to your friends. After you left that lab, you didn't go home because you were afraid to lead the scientists to your family."

Leon nodded curtly. He was staring down at his hands on the counter, and it was clear he didn't want to look at Callum. That was fine. Callum didn't need them to look at each other. He just needed Leon to do what he was comfortable with.

"I saw it in the lab, you know?" Leon said. "One of the other people there managed to escape. I was so fucking happy for her. I thought she would finally stop being hurt and that she'd bring someone back to help the rest of us. Instead, the hunters brought in a little girl."

Callum was sure he didn't want to hear what happened to that girl, but he didn't say anything. Instead, he picked up another piece of melon and stuck it into his mouth, knowing he was going to need a distraction to get through this story.

"The people in the lab knew who everyone they were experimenting on was. They had our names and addresses and knew about our families. They used them to threaten us and to make us obey, and for the most part, it worked." Leon sucked in a breath. "It worked because they made sure we knew what would happen when it didn't."

"Like with the little girl," Callum said softly.

"Yeah. She was that woman's sister. I guess the woman thought they were bluffing and that they'd never go after her family. I never saw her again, but I had to see that little girl for weeks. I know what she went through. I know how much pain she was in, how much the scientists and the guards enjoyed their revenge."

Leon suddenly looked up. His eyes blazed, but Callum wasn't afraid. He could never be afraid of Leon.

"I made sure they paid for every scratch they gave the little girl when I was released," Leon said. "I almost got killed because of that. When the enforcers opened my cage, I ran out toward the scientists and guards. Most of them had already been killed because they'd resisted arrest, but not all of them. I made sure they never left the facility."

Callum could see it. Leon wasn't a bad person. He was terrified and traumatized, and he'd gotten his revenge in the only way he knew how in a horrible situation. Callum would never blame him for that, just like he would never blame him for what he and the other mutants were doing.

Most people wouldn't take knowing their mate had taken many lives well. Even for Callum, it wasn't easy. Knowing his mate had killed people hadn't made him hesitate, though. It wasn't like Leon hurt any person off the street. He hurt monsters, people no one else tried to stop or who couldn't be stopped.

After what he and the other mutants had gone through, it would have been easy for them to lose their humanity. Sometimes, Callum wondered how they'd managed to cling to it during all that time. He didn't know, but he did know that they had and that now they were out, they were using what those scientists had done to them to help people. They were making sure that those scientists could never hurt anyone else.

Callum liked that. He didn't feel like he was in danger, even though he now knew about the labs. He was safe here in Fairview, with a bunch of trained mutants and other people around him. No one would be able to touch him here, but what about the people in the labs? What about people like that little girl who needed someone to protect her and didn't have it?

That was where Leon stepped in. It would have been so much easier for Leon to leave this life behind and hide, to try to forget everything that had been done to him, but instead, he was using his pain to help others. There was nothing sexier or more endearing, and at that moment, Callum knew how easy it would be to fall in love with his mate.

Leon was a complicated person, but then, wasn't everyone? Somehow, they'd find a way to make things work between them. Callum wouldn't have it any other way. But if they wanted things to work out, they needed to compromise. They needed ground rules that they'd both have to follow.

He leaned forward, but he didn't touch Leon, and not just because his hands were sticky with melon juice. He didn't want to startle him. "I'm not going to berate you for what you did. I don't care that you kill those scientists, hunters, and whoever else works in those labs. I don't think I could do it, but I don't see a problem with it."

Leon eyed Callum as though he expected him to break up with him or something. That was never going to happen, but Callum understood it would take Leon some time to believe it.

"And I don't need details about what happened to you in that lab," he continued. "If you want to tell me, I'll listen, but I'll never ask for it. I don't want you to have to live through that again. I already know you're traumatized and that you're working through all that pain and fear, and that's enough for me."

"But? Because I'm sure there's a *but*."

Callum grinned. "Eventually, there will be a butt and a dick."

Leon blinked, then laughed, and Callum laughed with

him, happy that he'd managed to do this. He needed to make Leon laugh and smile more. He needed to make him happy.

"But," Callum eventually said. "I need you to stop freaking out and believe I can care for myself. I know that you're afraid something will happen to me, just like something might happen to your brother. That's why you stayed away from him and the rest of your family, and while I'm not sure it was the right thing to do, it was your decision, and I'm not going to try to change your mind. There's a difference between your family and me, though. Actually, there are many of them. For one, I know about the hunters and the labs. I know what I need to protect myself from, and I'm ready to do so. I might not be as trained as you are, but I've been on my own for a long time. If things come to it, I can shift and fly away."

"You couldn't do it when that guy hit you with the bat."

"But I didn't expect it. I didn't know the hunters would be after me, and I wasn't on guard. I am now, even though I know that living in Fairview means I'm safe. I'm not going to let that knowledge make me less careful. Now that I know what's out there, I'm more careful, and not only because I don't want you to freak out. I don't want to be hurt. I don't want to end up in a lab. I want to live with you and be happy, and that means protecting myself." After finding out about the labs and the horror they created, it was impossible not to be careful, no matter where he lived.

Leon sighed. "I'll try, but I don't know how to do this."

"I don't need you to know how to do it. I just need you to try."

Leon didn't think Callum was lying. Any other person would have yelled at Leon for being overprotective. They would have run away and decided he was too much work.

But not Callum. Callum wanted to give Leon a chance. He

wanted them to be together and to be happy, to build a life. He knew that wasn't going to happen as long as Leon was freaking out about his safety, and he was trying to make Leon see that he didn't have to.

He was right. Most of the paranormal world didn't know about Fairview, and most of those who did had no idea where it was located. Once, Rikar had explained how they'd make that happen and how they kept the town safe, but Leon hadn't heard the entire explanation. He'd heard enough to know that the hunters would never find Fairview, and while that happened in his worst nightmares, it wasn't real.

What was real was in front of him, giving him a chance to make things right. Callum was offering Leon everything he could ever want, and while there were conditions, Leon was ready to compromise. It was the only way to make this work, and he desperately wanted it to.

He couldn't let his fear control him and, even worse, Callum. It wasn't fair, and he hated that he panicked so badly. He didn't know if anything could stop it, but he could certainly try harder than he had until now. After all, he got over his fear of something happening to his best friends. Their situation was worse because they went on raids, sometimes without him, although that didn't happen often. While they were working, he couldn't keep an eye on them, which meant they were at risk of getting hurt.

But that risk was there even when Leon was with them. Leon was only one man, and he wasn't perfect. Something could happen to any of the mutants, even if he was standing right next to them, and he needed to accept that. He also needed to accept that Callum was right and that he was safe in Fairview. He had to let Callum live his life and be free instead of smothering him with fear. He hoped he could and that it wouldn't end in disaster. He didn't know what he'd do if he lost Callum, but he wasn't planning on finding out.

He nodded. "I'll do everything you need me to do to make you happy."

"I don't need you to do anything but trust me."

Leon almost snorted. "I do trust you. I don't trust the rest of the world."

Callum tapped his fingertips on the counter. He was still plucking at the melon every so often, eating while he thought, and it was adorable. How had Leon ever lived without his mate? He didn't know, but he was sure that he wouldn't be able to continue living without him. He had no intention of trying, either. He hadn't been lying when he'd said he'd do anything Callum needed to be happy.

"You freak out when you don't know where I am because you think I could be hurt," Callum said slowly. "Right? That's why you panicked the other day when I was at lunch with Teddy and Hayes. You came here, couldn't find me, and had no idea where I was."

"I know it was stupid. I should've realized you were in town."

Callum flopped his hand. "It's not stupid or ridiculous. I'm just trying to understand. Your problem is that you don't know what's happening with me when you're not with me, but there's a fix for that."

Leon stared at his mate. He was pretty sure he knew what Callum was about to offer, and he wanted to say yes. He'd thought about it, and it would help soothe him. It would be the best way for him to be sure that Callum wasn't in pain or scared.

"If we bond, you'll be able to feel what I feel," Callum continued. "You'll know that I'm not afraid or hurt. That way, you'll be sure I'm safe."

Leon nodded. "It could work." He prayed it would, but he didn't want to make promises he might not be able to keep.

"I know it's a lot to ask, considering we just met. Most

people would tell you it's stupid to bond right away because you don't know me."

"I don't care what people think. If this is how things work and I make you happy, I'll do it."

Callum narrowed his eyes. "You need to think about it. You can't do this just because you think it will make me happy. I don't want you to regret this or resent me for pushing you into it. Maybe bonding because of your fears isn't the best way to start a relationship, but I don't think it matters. It's the best way for you to feel safe, and I want to give that to you, but only if you're sure you won't regret it."

Leon wanted to say yes right away, but he understood where Callum was coming from. This was a big decision for both of them, and they had to think about it.

Leon already had. He'd thought about bonding with Callum since he'd realized they were mates when Callum had been naked in the forest. Even then, without knowing Callum, Leon had wanted nothing more than to protect him.

He still did, and while Leon could protect him from the hunters or anything else that tried to attack him, the only way for him to protect Callum from *him* was to bond. That way, he'd always know that Callum was all right, and he wouldn't smother him with his fears and panic.

Leon hadn't thought Callum would want to do this so soon, but he did, and that was all Leon wanted, too. "I've already thought about it," he said, unable to look away from Callum. "I know what I want, and what I want is you."

Callum's cheeks flushed. Leon didn't think he'd ever seen him blush, but he loved it and wondered what he could do to make it happen again.

If things went the way they should, he'd have the rest of his life to find out.

"I can't promise I'll never regret this," Leon continued. "I don't think anyone can make that kind of promise about anything when it comes to relationships. We're mates, though, which means we're supposed to work. I think we can make each other happy as long as we try our hardest."

"That's all I want."

"I want the same. I'm sure I'll drive you nuts, and you'll yell at me and maybe not want to see me sometimes, but once we're bonded, that's it. We'll be one, and I'll know that even though you're angry at me, you're not scared or in pain."

This was the best way to make it work, and Leon was glad Callum realized that. He didn't think it would solve all his problems, but maybe that was something he could work on once he was sure Callum was safe. He didn't only have Callum in his life, after all. He had his friends, the people he considered his family, and he didn't want to smother them, either.

A wild hope took over. Maybe if he managed to get over his fear, he could even contact his family. He'd never allowed himself to think of it, but now, he couldn't stop himself from doing just that.

That was a problem for another day. Callum was Leon's present and the person he should focus on. Leon had the feeling that everything else would come eventually, and he couldn't wait, but right now, he also couldn't wait to bite Callum and make him his.

Callum stuffed the last piece of melon into his mouth, then licked his fingers. Leon couldn't look away, and he wondered if Callum was doing that on purpose. He might be, but even se, Leon didn't care. He even loved it a little.

"Right," Callum said. "I guess it's time for that butt and dick I mentioned earlier."

Leon burst out laughing. He never knew what to expect from Callum, but he always made him smile somehow. Maybe that was why they fit so well together. Leon had always been too serious, and what had happened to him had made it worse. He hadn't believed he had anything to smile about for a long time. He'd gotten over the worst of that before meeting Callum, but being with Callum gave him the push he needed to free himself from the last of the pain and finally allow himself to live.

He had a second chance. That wasn't something many people could say, and he'd been wasting it — or maybe not. Maybe he'd needed this time to heal. He wasn't like the old Leon yet and didn't think he ever would be, but he didn't *need* to be. Callum wanted him as he was, and Leon liked what he had become.

Callum grinned. He liked making Leon laugh and wanted to do it for the rest of his life. "What? Don't tell me you didn't think that."

"I didn't." Leon caught Callum's waist and pulled him closer. "But I love that you make me laugh."

"You can expect it and so much more from our life together."

Callum's heart turned into a puddle of goo at the expression on Leon's face. He tried not to let it show, then realized he didn't have a reason not to. Leon wanted him as much as he wanted Leon.

"I can't wait," Leon whispered.

"Neither can I. Today is the first day of our future together." Callum firmly believed that, and he wouldn't let anyone or anything convince him otherwise.

When he kissed Leon, Leon came easily, as if they'd been doing this for years. It felt familiar, yet at the same time, also brand new. Their souls recognized each other, but their brains and bodies had to catch up, and bonding would be a good way to make that happen. It would also help Leon deal with his fear, so as far as Callum was concerned, this was a win-

win situation. He got the guy and the bond, and Leon got a bond that would reassure him when he freaked out.

The bond would be a way for Leon to relax and let Callum in, and Callum wanted that more than anything.

They weren't in a rush as they headed upstairs. Callum made sure to give Max enough cuddles so that he wouldn't whine at his bedroom door. He usually slept there, too, and he wasn't used to Callum having company in his bed. Neither was Callum, but he was excited about having Leon there. They'd have to decide on how to deal with Max when they needed privacy, but Max didn't seem to have a problem being locked out because he didn't even get up from his spot on the floor by the stairs. Callum had several beds for him in the house, but no. Max usually slept on the floor.

Callum felt a bit awkward when they reached his bedroom. It had been a while since he'd slept with anyone, and never with someone as important to him and his future as Leon. He doubted there was anything he could do or say that would send Leon running, but making himself vulnerable made his stomach churn. This wasn't only physical. With Leon, it went so much deeper, and Callum wasn't used to sharing his feelings.

Of course, Leon was even worse at it, so he'd probably understand what Callum was feeling.

This wasn't the right moment to talk about feelings, even though they were about to bond. Callum didn't want to burden Leon today, of all days, but he wasn't sure he'd be able to hide how he felt while they made love. He was suddenly overwhelmed, and as soon as they reached his bedroom, he cleared his throat.

"I'll be right back," he said as he rushed to the bathroom. He didn't give Leon the time to say anything. He needed a few seconds to breathe and wrap his mind around what they were about to do.

He hadn't changed his mind. He still wanted to bond and believed it was a good idea. It was just a lot.

Once in the bathroom, he grabbed the edge of the sink and closed his eyes. He breathed in and out and ordered his racing heart to calm down, but the damn thing wouldn't listen, and neither would Callum's bat. He was excited about bonding with their mate, and Callum couldn't blame him. He was excited, too, so much so that he was panicking.

It was ridiculous.

Callum sucked in a breath, pushed away from the sink, and squared his shoulders. He wanted this, dammit. He wanted Leon, and he was going to make him his.

He opened the door and walked back into the bedroom, only to freeze.

Leon was naked in front of him as if it were the most natural thing in the world, and he was beautiful. Callum could see scars on his body, telling him about the places where the scientists had hurt him, but it was easy to ignore them. They represented Leon's past, while Callum was his future.

Leon held out a hand. "Come here."

Callum obeyed. He didn't even think about not doing it, and all the fear he'd been feeling seconds before was magically gone. He had no reason to be afraid of what was about to happen.

Leon took Callum's hand and guided him to the bed. Callum sucked in a breath as his back hit the mattress, and he tried to pull off his t-shirt, but Leon gently grabbed his wrists and pressed his arms into the sheets. Clearly, he wanted control right now, and the thought of his mate ordering Callum around made Callum's dick twitch in his jeans.

Leon let go of Callum's wrists, then leaned over him and pushed his t-shirt up to kiss his stomach. Callum sucked it in, but only for a few seconds. He figured Leon might as well see what he'd have in his bed for the next few decades. They both had to be themselves, bad self-esteem and defects included.

Callum was relieved that Leon didn't linger on his stomach, though. He kissed his way upward toward Callum's chest. His touch was so fucking light that Callum wanted to scream, but he wanted to give Leon what he needed more. He went with the flow, ready to withstand this torture for as long as Leon wanted.

He sighed in relief when Leon finally pulled his t-shirt off him. Leon's body was hard and muscled, while Callum's was softer, but it didn't seem to matter to either of them. Leon watched Callum as if he was precious, and he made Callum feel that way.

And all kinds of other ways as he continued exploring Callum's upper body with his lips and tongue. When he bit Callum's nipple, Callum's hips shot up before he could restrain himself. It made Leon chuckle, and he kissed Callum's nipple before continuing his torture.

Callum wasn't even naked yet, but he was already so close to coming that he was afraid he would as soon as Leon turned his attention to his cock. He undid his jeans and tried to wriggle out of them, even though he was sure Leon would try to stop him. He glared when Leon moved to do just that, and Leon raised his hands in surrender.

He laughed and helped Callum slide the rough fabric down his legs. Callum shivered and wondered if taking off his jeans had helped. He still wanted to come, dammit.

"There's lube in the nightstand," he told Leon.

Leon chuckled. "You're impatient, and I love it."

"Aren't you? Because I feel like my skin's crawling." He was more comfortable now that he was naked, but he was restless. They'd decided to bond, and he wanted to get to the point.

Leon leaned sideways to open the drawer. Callum was glad they were both on board. He grabbed his pillow, stuffed it under his ass, and opened his legs to give Leon easy access. They hadn't talked about who would be doing that, but Callum really hoped Leon would want to fuck him. He could fuck Leon once they recovered from their first time together.

"You're like a gift," Leon murmured as he ran a hand up Callum's leg.

"Eh, I'm not sure about that. That's why I want to bond with you. That way, you won't be able to run when you finally realize what you got yourself into."

Leon chuckled, but his expression was soft. "Never."

Callum wanted to believe him, and maybe he could allow himself to. Leon wasn't going anywhere, especially after they bonded, and Callum would be able to feel it soon.

"Together forever, right?" he asked.

Something passed in Leon's eyes, and he leaned over Callum to kiss him. He didn't have to answer for Callum to know this was it.

Callum wrapped his legs and arms around Leon. He wanted more, but he didn't want to rush his mate. This was a big moment for both of them.

But then he felt Leon's cock brush against his ass. He grinned like an idiot and tilted his hips, even though he knew he couldn't take Leon without prep. Maybe it would be enough to get Leon to finally get on with that.

Leon didn't let go of Callum. He moved his hips back, then forward again, sliding his cock between Callum's ass cheeks.

He was a fucking tease, and Callum loved it.

He didn't think anyone had ever taken care of him like this in the bedroom. Most of his hookups and boyfriends had been nice, but nothing like this. Leon took his time kissing and cuddling, and while the urgency of pleasure still crawled under Callum's skin, it was almost easy to ignore it when Leon was kissing him.

Callum was so utterly relaxed that he almost missed Leon

opening the lube he'd found in the nightstand. He opened his legs wider, sighing in pleasure when the first finger entered him.

It didn't hurt, even though it had been a while. Leon didn't rush this, either. It was as if he was trying to touch every inch of Callum's body, inside and out. Either that, or he was working hard on driving Callum nuts. The jury was still out.

The three little words he wanted to say were just there on his lips, but he swallowed them. He didn't want Leon to think he was only saying them because they were having sex. Sex didn't mean love, and neither did bonding. That didn't mean Callum wasn't falling for Leon, but he'd have time to tell him that. Besides, Leon would be able to feel it soon, so there was no need for Callum to say the words.

"Ready?" Leon asked.

It took everything Callum had not to take matters into his own hands and finally get Leon inside of him. "Yes."

He was ready to have Leon inside him and for him to be a part of him forever. He wanted Leon to feel what he felt and to know he was safe. He wanted to give him everything he'd refused himself since he'd been freed from the lab—safety, love, affection, laughter, and so much more.

He tensed when the head of Leon's cock breached him because no matter how thorough Leon had been, it was still a dick fitting in a tight space. Leon stopped moving and waited for Callum to be ready. Callum slapped his arm and glared at him. "Come on. Fuck me."

"I don't want to hurt you."

"You're not."

"Doesn't look like it."

"Some people like a little sting, Leon. I swear I'll stop you if it's too much." It never would be, but Callum didn't point that out because Leon was pressing forward again and giving him what he wanted, and it was perfect.

Callum felt every inch of him sliding inside him, and yes, it stung. He focused on the sensation of Leon above him and inside of him. It was corny, but sex had never felt like this. It wasn't only physical. Callum felt Leon in his body, mind, and heart, even though their bond wasn't complete yet.

"You feel so good," Leon murmured. "You don't know what you're giving me. I still can't believe you want this."

Callum caught Leon's face with his hands. "I do, so stop doubting this and me. Fuck me, Leon, and make me yours." Callum already was his, but Leon needed to be reminded of it.

Leon obeyed, and it was like Callum had imagined but also so much more. Leon took care of him, driving him higher and higher, and when Callum thought he'd finally fall, the feeling of fangs piercing his skin gave him a jolt. He cried out, and then he really was falling. Nothing existed in Callum's world except for Leon, and as Callum clung to him, he found himself jerking forward.

The taste of Leon's blood on his tongue and the meaning of the bite set Callum off. It was hard to drink Leon's blood while he was coming and unable to think, but he forced himself to focus.

He let go as soon as the bond between them snapped into place, and he flopped back against the mattress. Leon was moving more slowly now, and Callum screwed his eyes shut and reached out for him through their bond.

He could feel how much he mattered to Leon and how much at peace Leon finally was, and even though he hadn't had any doubts, he knew he'd made the right decision.

They were one, and they always would be.

CHAPTER FIVE

Callum had been right all along, and Leon wasn't afraid of admitting it. Callum had known that being bonded would help soothe Leon's fears, and that was what had happened. Now, Leon would know what Callum felt every minute of every day, so he'd immediately find out if something happened to him. At the first sign of fear or pain, he could grab Teddy and have him shimmer him to Callum.

Knowing that was surprisingly soothing. It had helped Leon deal with his fears, and while he still had to do so when it came to his friends and the other mutants, at least when it came to Callum, he wasn't freaking out every time Callum wasn't with him anymore.

That didn't mean everything was easy. When Leon didn't know where Callum was, there was always a moment of panic. His first thought was that the hunters had taken him, and while it only lasted for a few seconds, he didn't like that it happened at all. He'd been thinking about how to make sure it didn't, and he didn't think anyone would like the solution he'd come up with.

Killing every single hunter.

Eventually, Leon would get to do so with his friends' help. He hadn't mentioned any of this to them yet, and he wasn't planning to. For now, the only thing he wanted to do was focus on Callum and their new relationship.

Moore was planning the next raid to the lab where the people Callum had rescued were being taken. It had taken him a while to locate the place, because it was better hidden than most of the labs they'd dealt with. It would be tricky, and they might even need help from the council assassins, but Leon was happy to leave everything in Moore's hands. He knew what he was doing better than all of them.

Knowing he wouldn't have to go on a raid anytime soon had also helped Leon settle. It allowed him to focus on the new bond between him and Callum, which was what he was planning on doing. He wasn't sure how, so he needed to talk to his friends.

He'd texted Teddy to find out where he was, and since he'd used the group chat, Hayes had argued that he wanted to come, too. They'd agreed to meet at the coffee shop in town, and that was where Leon was headed.

There was a bounce in his step that had never been there. He was pretty sure he was smiling like an idiot, too, which wasn't something he was used to. He had no doubt his friends would tease him endlessly, but that was all right. He didn't mind being teased about Callum.

He knew his friends were relieved that he was finally dealing with his fear and everything else. They'd been worried and might still be, but they could see how happy Callum made Leon. Leon's life wasn't perfect, and it never would be, but being with Callum felt like taking the first step in the right direction, which was all Leon wanted.

When he'd been released from the lab, he'd never thought he'd have this. He'd wanted revenge, to hurt as many people as the people who had hurt him, and he'd never thought he could be happy again. He'd been in too much pain, and his hate had been deep. He hadn't thought it would ever vanish, and it hadn't, but the feeling wasn't as strong as it had been before. As long as he didn't think about his past, it was fairly easy to ignore it. That wouldn't be the case forever, but Leon was glad for the respite. He'd have to see how to deal with all of this once he was back at work, but as long as Moore was still working on his plan, that wouldn't happen.

Leon could focus on his mate.

He pushed open the coffee shop door and looked around. Hayes was already sitting at a table, sipping his drink, but Teddy wasn't there yet. Leon waved at Hayes, then went to order a drink for him and Teddy. If they were cold by the time Teddy arrived, it would mean Teddy was late, and Leon wouldn't hesitate to point that out.

It only took a few minutes for their coffees to be ready, and when Leon joined Hayes at the table, Teddy had arrived. He made grabby hands for his coffee in a gesture that reminded Leon of Callum so much that Leon found himself smiling.

"I know that look," Teddy said. "You're in *love*."

He was teasing, but there was no cruelty in it. He was happy for Leon, just like he'd been happy for Hayes when he'd met Rikar.

Leon flopped in his seat. "Yeah, I am," he admitted.

Teddy blinked as if he hadn't expected the admission. "So you and Callum talked? You've looked happier lately, but I was too afraid to ask and ruin everything."

"We did much more than talk."

Leon wiggled his eyebrows, then reached for his sweater and pulled the collar away from his neck. It exposed the bite on his neck, and the reaction from both Teddy and Hayes was enough to make it worth it. He normally wouldn't have exposed himself like this, but they were his best friends.

They both got up and came around the table to hug Leon, smothering him with love. He laughed and clung to them, screwing his eyes shut. He couldn't lose this. He couldn't lose any of the mutants, but especially not his best friends and Callum. He'd do everything he had to in order to make sure these three people were always safe and happy.

Eventually, Teddy and Hayes sat back in their chairs. Teddy leaned forward, his eyes glinting in happiness. "You're not going to give us details, are you?"

"I'm not," Leon confirmed. "Callum suggested bonding because he thought it would help me not panic when he isn't with me, and he was right. He's not here, but I can feel he's sleepy and happy, so I know he's fine."

Teddy nodded. "Makes sense. I'm glad he could see this would help you and that neither of you balked. It can't be easy to decide to bond so soon after you met."

"It was the easiest decision I've ever made. I knew I wanted to bond with Callum from the first time I saw him. I was already smothering him enough, though, which was why I didn't bring it up." But Leon was glad that Callum had.

"So now that you're a bonded man, how are things going?" Hayes asked.

"Better than I could have imagined."

"I want that, too," Teddy said as he pouted. "When's my turn going to come?"

"Probably soon. Everyone around here is finding their mate."

That brought the smile back to Teddy's face. "Right. I just have to wait."

Leon hoped for Teddy's sake that his mate was coming. He deserved it, just like every mutant did. After everything they'd gone through, they should have all the happiness in the world.

"Will you be moving in with him?" Hayes asked.

"Yeah. I need to talk to the others, but they'll be happy for me." Leon lived with Teddy and a bunch of other mutants. He was close to all of them, although not as close as he was to Teddy and Hayes, but they'd understand.

All of them had a second chance at life. It wasn't the life they'd imagined they'd have, and it wasn't always easy, but none of them would waste this opportunity. Leon certainly wouldn't. Now that he and Callum were bonded, he wanted to be with his mate more than ever.

"I want to spoil him," he said. "I'm just not sure how to do it."

"Fruit," Teddy declared.

Leon laughed. It was good to see that his friends already knew Callum so well, although Callum had never made a secret of how much he loved fruit. He said it was because he was a fruit bat, but Leon wasn't convinced that was the case.

"Take him on a picnic," Hayes said. "You can grab fruit, relax, maybe shift, and have fun. I'm sure he'd like that. Besides, eventually, Moore will have more work for us, and we won't have as much time to spend with our mates as we do now. We should take advantage of it while we can."

He was right. Leon didn't want to waste time, so after spending half an hour with his friends, he left them at the coffee shop and headed to the grocery store. By now, the people who worked here knew why he was there, so they weren't surprised to see him leave the store with a bulging bag of fruit. The way they waved and smiled at him made him feel like he was part of this town, and he liked it more than he'd expected.

Fairview was his new home. He'd known he would settle down here because it was the safest place for him, but he hadn't expected to actually like it.

He crossed through the parking lot on his way to the small street on which Callum lived. As he walked past a van, a hand shot out and grabbed his face, covering his mouth. He dropped his bag of fruit and turned to fight his attacker, but something heavy hit him on the side of the head, making him see stars for long enough that the attacker managed to stuff him into the back of the van.

Shit. He'd been terrified something like this would happen to Callum, but instead, it was happening to him.

Leon had texted Callum a while ago, telling him to get ready because he was picking him up. He hadn't told Callum what he was planning, but Callum was always excited to spend time with his mate. Today wasn't any different, and as he watched the minutes tick by, he wondered what Leon had come up with this time.

Things between them had been going incredibly well. Callum had never believed he'd regret bonding with Leon, and he wouldn't. He hadn't been sure how Leon would react to his suggestion, but he'd only been half surprised when Leon had said yes. No matter the circumstances or their pasts, they were mates, and that was what mattered the most. Leon wanted Callum as much as Callum wanted him.

Callum had never imagined he could be so happy, but he was, and he didn't think he'd ever regret moving to Fairview and giving Leon a chance. Things could still change between them, but Leon was making a visible effort, and Callum loved him for that. He didn't know if he was in love with him yet, but eventually, he would be, and that didn't scare him one bit.

Why should it? Why should he be afraid of falling in love with his mate, of all people? He could see they would work well together no matter how hard things were.

They had to.

Callum called him when ten minutes had passed, and Leon still hadn't arrived. He didn't want to appear needy, but Leon had said he'd be there in five minutes, and Callum wanted to know what was keeping him.

He had his phone in hand when he felt shock run through the bond he shared with Leon. It was so strong that he felt like he couldn't breathe for a moment. It didn't last long, but it was enough to freak him out.

Why was Leon shocked? He'd been meeting with Teddy and Hayes, and while he hadn't told Callum what he was planning for their outing, it shouldn't be anything that would shock him. Maybe there had been an accident, and that was what had shocked Leon, but right after that emotion, Callum felt other things. They came fast, almost not giving him time to try to identify them.

It was odd that he knew what he was feeling, even though he wasn't the one feeling it. He could tell that Leon was worried and a bit afraid, very much annoyed and angry. Callum couldn't make sense of the situation because he didn't know what was happening, but his emotions were enough to tell him something had happened.

He wasn't surprised when Leon didn't answer his phone. It was ringing, but he wasn't sure if that was good or bad. Since Leon had been with Teddy and Hayes, they were who Callum called next.

It only took Teddy a few rings to answer. "Hey. I thought you and Leon would be out already."

"Do you know what he was planning?"

"Was?" Teddy's voice lost its bubbliness. "Does that mean he never got to you?"

"He didn't, even though he texted that he was almost here. I also felt some weird stuff through our bond." Callum didn't know if Leon had told his friends they were bonded, but he didn't care.

"Dammit."

"Do you think something happened? You're not with him anymore?"

"No, he left a little while ago. He was going to the grocery store. I'm going to find him, all right?"

"No." Callum desperately wanted to say yes, but what if this was part of Leon's plan? Without knowing what his plan was, it was impossible to know how Leon would feel about it.

Maybe he was being dramatic. He'd been annoyed at Leon for worrying that something had happened to him every time he was out of his sight, and now, he was the one doing it. Leon would be pissed if this ruined whatever plans he had.

Callum understood better what Leon had gone through when he hadn't found him the other day. He didn't want to give in to the panic, but it wasn't easy. He told himself to breathe and prodded at the bond at the back of his mind, hoping that Leon's situation had changed.

"He's mostly annoyed," he said slowly. "A bit scared, too, but there's also a good amount of trust in the way he feels at the moment."

"Probably because he knows we'll come after him. I have to go, Callum."

"Where was he headed when he left?"

"The grocery store."

Callum hadn't expected that, but maybe he should have. Leon had been spoiling him by bringing him fruit almost every day. It wasn't anything special, yet at the same time, it was. It showed that Leon knew Callum and that he wanted to make him happy.

And he did, so much. Callum wanted to do the same for him, which meant giving him trust.

"Why don't we meet there?"

"It would be better if I just shimmered to him. I could already have gone and been back by now."

Callum heard someone else speak, probably Hayes. Callum was dying to know what he was saying, but Teddy wasn't making it easy on him.

Teddy came back on the line, huffing. "Fine. Hayes agrees with you and says that we should meet at the grocery store."

Callum was surprised but grateful. "It's probably nothing. We shouldn't worry too much before we know if something is going on."

"By the time we do, it might be too late," Teddy snapped. He sucked in a breath. "I'm sorry. I didn't mean to snap, and

I'm not angry at you. I'm just worried for my friend."

"I'm worried about him, too, and if something did happen to him, then you absolutely need to go get him."

"Hayes said that we need to be careful, and he's right. I can't just shimmer to Leon without knowing what's going on with him. He's probably in danger, but that doesn't mean I should put myself and anyone else coming with me in danger, too. He'd never forgive me if something happened to you."

"Nothing is going to happen to me."

Callum couldn't deny he was terrified for Leon. He wanted to believe that nothing had happened and that he was about to arrive, but he doubted that was the case. He'd felt the fear and shock. He could still feel the turmoil in Leon's mind. He wanted to go to his rescue but wasn't trained to do things like that. Teddy and Hayes were, and if Hayes thought they should wait to see what was going on, then it probably was the right thing to do.

They hung up, and Callum rushed out of the house after saying goodbye to Max. He could've had Teddy pick him up, but the grocery store was so close that it probably would have taken as long as it took him to run there.

When he reached the store, he wasn't surprised to see Teddy and Hayes were already in the parking lot. As he watched, Teddy walked inside. Callum ran to Hayes, hoping he'd have more answers. "Do you know anything new?"

Hayes shook his head. His expression was grim, but that didn't mean there wasn't hope.

"Teddy went inside to talk to the owner. You and I are going to look through the parking lot."

It didn't take them long to find something. The first clue was a squished orange. Clearly, a vehicle had run it over, and when Callum followed the trail, he found more fruit. It led him to a bag abandoned in the middle of the parking lot, and he stared at it for a moment, trying to understand what it meant.

Leon had gone to the grocery store. He'd bought fruit for Callum and had started to walk toward his house. He'd been stopped in the parking lot and dropped the bag.

Callum poked at their bond again, and to his surprise, a wave of reassurance came through. It was strong enough that it almost knocked him to his knees, but he stayed on his feet, closing his eyes for a moment.

"He's all right," he said.

Both Hayes and Teddy were in front of him when he opened his eyes. "What do you know?" Teddy asked.

"Nothing for sure. I can just feel him trying to reassure me, and while he's scared, it's not the strongest emotion he's feeling right now. I think he's more annoyed than anything."

Which didn't make sense if he'd been kidnapped like it looked like he had. What the fuck was happening?

Leon was never going to live this down. It wouldn't be Callum making fun of him. No, Callum was scared and frantic, and from what Leon could feel, he just wanted Leon to come home. Leon had no doubt that the same went for his friends, but once they knew he was all right, they'd make fun of him forever.

After telling Callum to be careful so many times, after freaking out over him going around town on his own because something might happen to him, something had happened to *Leon*. He was trained and a mutant, yet he'd been kidnapped.

He really fucking hated himself right now.

He had no idea what was happening. After he'd been pushed into the van, still trying to recover from the blow to his head, he'd been blindfolded and tied. He was pretty sure that if he tried, he could get out of the ties. They didn't feel tight, and it was almost as if the person who'd tied him had done a half-hearted job.

From the sounds around him, he suspected the person who'd hit him was the same person who'd tied him up and was now driving the van. There seemed to only be one of them, which didn't make sense when it came to hunters. They were so scared of shifters attacking them that they traveled in packs, behaving like the animals they accused shifters of being. They would never attack a shifter on their own, especially if they wanted to hand over that shifter to a lab.

That was the only thing that made sense. If this hunter had wanted to hurt Leon, it would have been easy. He wouldn't even have had to leave the parking lot. He certainly wouldn't have had to tie Leon up and blindfold him, then drive away. That meant that this hunter wanted something from Leon, and there was only one thing hunters wanted from shifters.

To sell them.

The thought made Leon's skin crawl, but he knew things wouldn't get that far this time around. He wasn't powerless anymore. Even more importantly, people knew something had happened to him, and they'd come to his rescue if he couldn't rescue himself. He didn't care how much Teddy laughed at him. He wanted to see his best friend's face and reassure Callum.

They had to be frantic right now. Leon had no doubt that Callum had already contacted Teddy and Hayes. He would have felt the shock Leon felt when he was taken, as well as the fear and everything else. The last thing Leon wanted was to scare him, but he couldn't do anything about the way he felt. That was why he tried to send reassurance down their bond, hoping Callum would understand that he was all right.

Leon wasn't surprised that Teddy hadn't shimmered to him yet. No matter how much he cared about Leon, he'd been trained not to act on impulse, especially in this kind of situation. If Leon had to guess, Teddy and Hayes were on their way to talk to Moore. He was their leader, which meant that if something needed to be done, he'd be the one to decide what that something was.

Leon wasn't afraid to be left behind. More than coworkers or team members, the mutants were a tight-knit family, and Moore would never leave any of them behind, or as it was, in the hands of the hunters. Still, it would take some time for him and the others to arrive, and Leon didn't want to just sit around and do nothing as he waited.

He cleared his throat. "Hey," he said. "What's going on? Why did you take me?"

The only answer he got was a grunt. He hadn't been a hundred percent sure that his kidnapper was a man, although that was what it had felt like when they'd struggled, but now, he knew it. The voice belonged to a man.

That didn't help Leon find out what the man wanted.

"If you plan on selling me to one of those labs, I don't think you'll get much money for me. They already had me. I'll be useless for their experiments."

There still was no answer, but the hunter sucked in a breath. It felt almost as if he wanted to talk but didn't allow himself to.

Leon settled back against the side of the van, wondering what else he could do. Should he try to escape? If he was being taken to a lab, it might be a good idea to find out where that lab was. The only way to do that would be to stay where he was, even though he wasn't happy about it. He didn't want to be tied up like a salami in the back of the van. He wanted to be with his mate, playing and eating fruit, dammit.

The van screeched to a stop, sending Leon rolling. He swore and tried to get back into a sitting position, but it wasn't easy since his hands were tied. By the time he managed, the van's back doors had opened, and a hand touched his shoulder.

He jerked back. He had no intention of making this easy on the hunter. If they were at one of the labs, the hunter would have help to get Leon out, but Leon was ready to fight. He wouldn't allow anyone to take him from Callum. He wouldn't allow anyone to take his happiness.

When fingers touched his cheek, he jerked away. The hunter made an impatient sound, and Leon almost told him to fuck off.

"If you stay still, I can take the blindfold off," the hunter said.

Leon was tempted to resist but wanted to see where they were and what was happening, so he obeyed. His skin crawled as the fingers touched him again, but thankfully, the hunter made quick work of the blindfold. He pulled it from Leon's eyes, and Leon quickly blinked, needing to know where he was.

He didn't know. The van was parked in front of a house that had seen better days. Leon couldn't say it was abandoned, but it wasn't in the best shape. One of the windows on the ground floor was broken, and the porch sagged to one side. The area around the house was a mess of plants and wildflowers, and the driveway on which the van was parked was cracked. In the distance, Leon could see other houses, but they were too far away for anyone to notice what was happening there.

At least he wasn't in a lab. The hunter couldn't do any experiments in a place like this, which meant there was a chance for Leon to get out in one piece.

He sat up straighter and raised his hands. "Any chance you'll take this off, too?"

The hunter hesitated. He was younger than Leon had expected. Usually, hunters were anywhere between their late thirties and early fifties. Leon had seen a few women, but they were almost always men, and it was usually obvious that life hadn't been tender with them. The guy standing in front of him didn't strike him like a hunter, even though that had to be the case.

Right? Why else would this guy have kidnapped him?

But he didn't look anything like a hunter. He was on the short side and looked like he hadn't had a good meal in a while. His blond hair and clothes were dirty, and he kind of smelled, which added to the impression that he wasn't taking care of himself. He wore jeans and an old sweater too big for him, and he appeared young, maybe in his twenties.

His appearance gave Leon an impression of fragility and of not being used to doing what he was doing. It didn't mean he wasn't dangerous, even if that was the case. Hunters always were, and while there was nothing that indicated this guy was a hunter, there also wasn't anything that indicated that he wasn't. There had to be a reason he'd grabbed Leon of all people, which meant he probably knew that Leon was a shifter or maybe even that he could heal. It was common knowledge in Fairview but not beyond it. The only people who would know would be hunters or scientists who'd escaped a raid.

"I'll take it off only if you promise to help me," the hunter said.

Leon snorted. "Why would you need my help?"

"To heal my brother."

"I'm going with them," Callum declared, glaring at Moore.

"You're not trained for this," Moore said, clearly trying to be the voice of reason.

"I don't care. I'm not letting them go alone. Besides, we don't even know what's happening. Leon is probably fine, and I'm making a mess out of this."

"You don't really believe that, and neither do I. Leon wouldn't *not* come when he had plans with you. You matter to him."

Moore was right, but Callum didn't want to admit it. He wasn't fragile, dammit. He might not be trained, but he could be useful in a fight — if that was what they were about to walk in on.

He crossed his arms over his chest. "I'm sorry, but I *am* going with them, whether you like it or not."

"I don't like it, but I can see it's useless to try to convince you to stay back." Moore turned to Teddy and Hayes. "I can send more people with you."

Teddy shook his head. "From what Callum has been feeling through the bond, I don't think we have to worry about what we'll find once we reach Leon. Even if he's been taken by hunters, Hayes and I can get rid of them while Callum focuses on Leon. He hasn't felt any pain from Leon yet, which probably means Leon is fine. He could have been tied up or something like that, and if Callum frees him, he can help us fight."

Callum wasn't going to say *he* could help them fight, too, because he was pretty sure he couldn't. He'd never had to fight physically, and he hoped he wasn't going to have to learn to do so now. He just wanted his mate back and for Leon to be fine.

Moore sighed. "Fine. Go and grab Leon. We'll be waiting for you here, but if we don't see you soon, I'm sending Rikar after you."

Callum wanted to grumble that it wasn't fair because Rikar wasn't trained, either, but he was a Nix. He could shimmer more mutants to them in case Hayes and Teddy needed the help. Hopefully, they wouldn't because if they did, it would mean they'd walked into a trap and that Leon was in trouble.

Callum's mouth was dry as he watched Teddy nod, then stretch out his arms. Hayes didn't hesitate to take one of his hands, and Callum quickly mirrored his movement. Their expressions were stoic, but he couldn't help but wonder if they were as scared as he was. Maybe they'd done this so many times that they didn't feel that way anymore. Maybe for them, this was just routine.

Callum almost wished he could say the same.

But for him, it wasn't routine. He'd never experienced it, and he was already worried about Leon. Having to go into a situation like this wasn't helping, but he wasn't staying back, so he clung to Teddy's hand. Teddy watched him for a moment, and Callum nodded at him, hoping he would understand.

He did. He shimmered them without arguing that Callum should stay back. Callum barely had the time to wonder what they'd walk in on that they were already there, and he quickly looked around, trying to find out if they were in danger.

He had no idea where they were, but it looked like a bedroom, even though the only piece of furniture was a dusty bed. The mattress was bare, and a man was stretched out on top of it.

That was all Callum managed to see before the situation turned into chaos. A man cried out and rushed toward them. Callum took a step back, relieved when Teddy moved in front of him. His stance told Callum that he'd defend him no matter what happened.

That was when Callum's gaze found Leon. He was leaning over the man on the bed, or at least he had been. He straightened, and his eyes went wide. He seemed to be all right, but Callum wouldn't be convinced of that until he got his hands on him.

Just then, the hunter reached Teddy. Teddy punched him in the face, sending him stumbling back. The man looked dazed and stunned, as if he hadn't expected the punch.

"Stop," Leon ordered.

Everyone froze. The only sound Callum could hear was the

heavy breathing coming from the man on the bed. It made him wonder what had happened to him, but he hesitated to step away from Teddy. He desperately wanted to check in on Leon, but this felt like it might be dangerous.

"I'm fine," Leon said. "Perseus hasn't hurt me."

"Perseus?" Teddy asked as if he couldn't make sense of the name.

Leon gestured at the man Teddy had punched. "He's Perseus. His brother here is Orion."

Perseus was still rubbing his jaw, but he looked sheepish. "Our mother liked constellations," he mumbled.

Teddy looked bewildered, but Callum didn't care about the guy's name. He pushed past him, rushing toward Leon. Leon's eyes widened when he saw him, and he opened his arms, allowing Callum to throw himself into them.

Leon was fine. He wasn't hurt. He didn't even sound worried, and that was enough for Callum to relax. He might not know what was happening, but Leon would tell them.

"You're okay," Hayes said.

"I'm fine," Leon confirmed. "But Orion isn't. He needs my help, so I'm going to heal him before I can explain what happened."

Teddy grunted as if he disagreed with that decision but didn't try to stop Leon. Leon let go of Callum and leaned over Orion again, gently touching his forearm. Now that Callum was getting a better look at the man, he could see something was truly wrong with him.

The two brothers looked like each other, even though Orion was much taller and bigger. He was sickly pale, though, and one of his hands clutched his ribs as if they were broken. Callum winced at the memory of his own ribs being cracked. He remembered that pain all too well, so he hoped Leon would be able to help Orion.

"I can help," Teddy muttered as he pushed past Perseus.

He stumbled but quickly got himself together and turned back to Leon.

Leon's eyes were closed, and he was focused on Orion. "He has several broken ribs, and one of them punctured his lung," he explained without looking at Teddy. "He's lost a lot of blood, and it's still all inside of him."

Callum didn't fully understand how Leon's healing thing worked. He wasn't even sure Leon understood it. The only people who might be able to explain it were the ones who'd changed Leon, but Callum doubted Leon would ever ask them about it. They were probably dead, anyway.

It was a miracle that Leon could do this. Even though it sounded incredibly complicated and like Orion would be better off at the hospital, Leon was going to heal him. He wouldn't even try if he wasn't convinced he could do it, which meant that he could.

Teddy pressed a hand to Orion's chest, making him groan. Perseus tried to go to him, but Hayes stopped him, gently pushing him back. Teddy's hand glowed, and while Leon's didn't, it was clear he was healing Orion.

Callum held his breath as he watched the scene. He wasn't sure how long it took, but no more than a few minutes. It was longer than when Leon had healed him, which was enough to tell him how complicated it was. Leon wouldn't have let Teddy help him otherwise.

But eventually, both Leon and Teddy leaned back. Orion wasn't as pale, and he groaned as he opened his eyes. Perseus cried out and rushed to his brother. This time, Hayes allowed him to go.

"Is he healed?" Hayes asked.

"He's perfectly fine," Leon confirmed. He looked tired, but nothing that would tell anyone what he'd just done. It was incredible.

"Good," Teddy said as he grabbed both the brothers and

shimmered them away, leaving Hayes, Leon, and Callum where they were.

Leon sighed. "I knew he was going to do that."

"Do you blame him?" Hayes asked. "They kidnapped you."

"Only Perseus did, and it was because his brother needed help."

Callum shook his head. "While I understand why he did it, he could have just asked. You would have done it."

"Not for a hunter."

"Are we sure they're hunters? How did they know about Fairview?"

Leon pressed his lips together. "I don't know, but I'm sure Moore will find out."

Callum had no doubt he would. He just hoped Moore wouldn't go too hard on the brothers, especially Orion.

CHAPTER SIX

The worst had happened, and everyone had survived.

That was what Leon kept telling himself since he'd come back from being kidnapped. Before, he'd been afraid that Callum would be taken from him, but instead, he'd been the one taken. He'd come out of it in one piece and unhurt, and while it had been scary, knowing that the worst had happened without anyone getting hurt had helped him relax. That, coupled with the bond he and Callum shared, was enough to feel like he could finally let go of his fears.

It was the first time he'd felt that way since he'd left the lab. He didn't know where it would take him, but he hadn't been able to stop thinking about contacting his family, especially his brother. He and Anthony had always been close, even though Anthony was much younger than Leon. Since shifters lived so long, it wasn't unheard of for a mated couple to have children more than thirty or forty years apart. Anthony was only seven and still a little boy, which was one of the reasons Leon had been so afraid something would happen to him. Now, he knew that even if something did, it didn't mean he would get hurt. Leon would go after him, as would everyone else in his new family. They'd protect Anthony and Leon's parents, just like they protected the families of the other mutants.

"You've been particularly quiet today," Callum said.

Leon peered down at him. They were supposed to be watching a movie, and Callum had settled in with his head on Leon's thigh, but he wasn't looking at the TV. He was looking up at Leon instead, and Leon found himself smiling down at him. He ran his fingers through Callum's hair, loving how Callum made an almost purring sound.

"I was thinking about what happened," Leon explained.

Callum grimaced. "I don't think I've ever been so scared in my life. I mean, I was scared when I was attacked, but it wasn't the same. I guess that now, I understand how you feel."

Leon wished he wouldn't, but there was no going back. What was done was done, and Callum would never be able to forget what he'd gone through when he'd realized Leon was gone. Leon would do whatever it took to make Callum feel better about it, though.

"Perseus wasn't planning to hurt me."

"I don't care what he was planning. He kidnapped you instead of asking you to help. And we still don't know how he found out about Fairview."

Perseus was refusing to talk about anything that wasn't his brother, while Orion had been in too much pain to know what was happening. It made an already complicated situation even more complicated, but Leon trusted Moore to untangle it.

After Teddy had shimmered Perseus and Orion to Fairview, he'd come back for Hayes, Leon, and Callum. He'd told them that he'd dumped the brothers with Moore, and by the time they were back, Moore had locked them up in one of the cells. They weren't comfortable, and Leon felt slightly guilty. Even though he was pretty sure the brothers were hunters, they hadn't hurt him. To be honest, they didn't look like they could hurt a fly, even though Orion was large.

To everyone's surprise, he seemed to be the gentler of the two. Perseus was angry and never missed a chance to tell anyone who walked into his cell about it, but that was when he stopped talking. He wouldn't give Moore any kind of information about himself or his brother, and Leon didn't know how this would end.

It was none of his business. Perseus had kidnapped him, which meant he shouldn't care what happened to him. He'd seen how the brothers had lived in that house, though. More importantly, he'd seen how much Perseus had cared about his brother. It had reminded him of Anthony, especially after he'd found out that Orion was younger. Perseus and Orion weren't that many years apart, but Perseus still cared for his little brother the way Leon always had. It had touched something in Leon, and he wanted to help.

But not right now. He had other things to focus on right now, like Callum, who was still staring up at him.

"I don't think they're dangerous," Leon said with a sigh.

"I agree."

Leon frowned. "I thought you were angry."

"I can be pissed that Perseus kidnapped you and believe he didn't mean any harm at the same time. He was an idiot, but he was trying to save his brother. I'm pretty sure he panicked and thought you wouldn't help him if he just came to you, especially if you found out he was a hunter."

"He wouldn't have been wrong. If he had come up to me and told me about his brother, my first thought would have been to contact Moore."

"Which is why he decided to kidnap you." Callum wrinkled his nose. "It was kind of stupid."

"That's one way to describe it. Thankfully, it's over." Leon leaned over to kiss Callum's forehead. He had to scrunch into an odd position, but that didn't stop him.

Nothing would stop him from kissing Callum.

"So, now you've been kidnapped," Callum said. "And I haven't been."

"There's no need to remind me of that. I'm aware of what happened."

"I wasn't trying to remind you. I was just thinking about what it means."

Leon grinned. He wasn't surprised that Callum had been thinking about it as much as he had. Callum knew that now that they were together, there was only one thing that Leon wanted.

To see his family again.

"And what does it mean?" Leon asked.

Callum sat up. "It's not funny when you act like you don't know what I'm talking about. Your family. Your brother. When are you going to contact them?"

Leon didn't have an answer and didn't even know what he'd do. "I'm not sure it's the best idea."

Callum threw his hands in the air. "What are you talking about? You know that if they ever need anything, the entire group of mutants will volunteer. They'll help you in any way they can, so you don't have to worry about the hunters going after them anymore."

"I think I'll worry about that for the rest of my life."

Callum's tone softened. "Which is understandable, but it still doesn't mean you should stay away from them. You've been doing so for too long, and it's not fair to you or to them."

"They probably think I'm dead. It's been three years, and Anthony barely knew me. He won't recognize me, and even if he does, is it fair to do that? Wouldn't it be better to leave them alone? They've already grieved me."

"Don't you think they would want to know that you're alive? They might have grieved your loss, but I have no doubt they'd be happy to find out they did so for nothing. I'm sure they'd rather have you in their life."

Callum was right. When Leon tried to put himself into the position his parents were in, he could admit that he'd want anyone related to him to be alive if he thought they were dead. Besides, his parents had never known what had happened to him, so maybe they weren't done grieving. They weren't done hurting because they didn't have a body or an explanation, and that was something Leon could help with. Wouldn't it be selfish for him not to?

"I might still put them in danger," he murmured.

"So what? Ask them if they want to move to Fairview. Do you really think they'd say no after getting you back? You can explain everything that happened to you and tell them why you stayed away. I'm sure they'll be pissed, but they'll want the same thing you do."

Leon wanted to be with his family, and he knew they felt the same, or rather, that they would if they knew he was alive. The thought of them moving to Fairview wasn't bad, and Leon wasn't sure why he hadn't thought about it before.

Maybe he'd been too stuck in his spiral of fear and panic, but he wasn't anymore. He never would be again because he had Callum, Teddy, Hayes, and the rest of their family. Maybe soon, he could have his parents and Anthony, too.

But to make that happen, he would have to be brave. He would have to ignore his fear and do the thing he'd been avoiding for years.

Callum had never blamed Leon for being afraid, but after what they'd gone through recently, he understood how important it was for Leon to keep his family safe. He didn't want to push him into doing something he wasn't comfortable with, but it was clear that he missed his family deeply, and it didn't feel fair for them to still be separated. All of Leon's worries were valid, but that didn't mean they couldn't find a way around them. Callum was sure they could. If Leon let him, he'd find a way to make it work.

Since he didn't want to push, he let it go—for now. Leon was thinking about what Callum had said, and that was enough. No matter what conclusion he came to, Callum would support him. He would love to have Leon's family move to Fairview and meet his parents and brother, but even if it never happened, he'd make sure Leon was happy. Leon deserved it, and who better than Callum to give it to him?

Callum tried to focus on the movie, but with Leon so close, it was hard. He could feel the tension in Leon's body, so he knew Leon was thinking about this and probably about what had happened with the constellation brothers. Maybe it would have been better if Callum had been kidnapped. That way, he would have been able to show Leon that he could defend himself. He wasn't as useful as Leon when it came to healing people. No one was.

Callum hadn't heard anything new about the brothers and was curious. What had happened to them? Why had Orion been wounded? How had Perseus found the village when only a handful of people who didn't live here were supposed to know its location? The more questions Callum thought of, the more he wanted to go see them. Orion might not be able to tell him much, but Perseus should.

If he was willing, which he hadn't been until now.

"Do you know if Moore is the only one who interrogated the brothers?" he asked.

"You mean the hunters?"

"Yeah."

"As far as I know. It's his job since he's in charge."

That made sense, but maybe that was why Perseus wasn't talking. Maybe he didn't like Moore or was afraid of him. Maybe he wasn't willing to put his brother or anyone else in danger more than he already had, and he felt like talking to Moore would do just that.

"Has Moore thought about asking someone else to talk to them?"

"What are you planning?" Leon asked, sounding

suspicious.

Callum laughed. Even though they hadn't been together that long, his mate knew him well. "I was just wondering. Maybe they're afraid of him, and that's why they're not talking."

"I can't deny Moore is intimidating, especially when he's focusing on hunters, but we're not going to braid their hair and give them cookies. They're prisoners. What do you expect us to do? Hold their hands and tell them everything will be okay?"

"I don't know. Maybe it would give you what you're looking for, though."

Leon snorted. "They're not talking because they're hunters. They hate us, and they were probably planning to attack the village. They have to be scouts sent by their people, and as long as we keep them, they won't be able to give the others any information."

What Leon was saying made sense, but something bothered Callum. "We still don't know how they found the village."

"Which is why we're never letting them go."

Callum's stomach churned. He knew what the mutants did and didn't blame them for killing the scientists and the other bad guys they found in the labs. Those people were monsters, and Callum understood the need to make sure they would never hurt anyone ever again. From what he'd been told, the mutants gave everyone they found a choice. Either they surrendered, or they paid with their lives. He'd thought most people agreed to surrender, but Leon had told him that wasn't the case. They were too scared of what the council would do to them if they did, so they usually tried to fight their way out of the situation.

It seldom worked.

But this was different. They weren't talking about

scientists. It was true that the hunters had done horrible things, too, but had Orion and Perseus? They knew nothing about the two brothers, and the only reason Perseus had kidnapped Leon was that he'd needed him to save his brother. Otherwise he wouldn't have grabbed Leon, and no one would ever have known about them.

But they would have known about the village. They needed answers, and what the mutants were doing wasn't working.

Callum pushed into a sitting position and twisted to face Leon. His mate's wary expression probably meant that he knew he wouldn't like what Callum was about to suggest. Well, tough luck. If he was going to be with Callum, he better get ready to listen to things he didn't like.

"We should talk to them," Callum said.

Leon started shaking his head before Callum was even done speaking. "You're not talking to anyone."

"Then it's going to be a bit hard for me to continue living in the village."

Leon rolled his eyes. "You know what I mean. Why would you want to talk to them? They're hunters. A hunter tried to kidnap you, remember? He hurt you."

"He did, but I'm fine. Besides, you took care of that guy. Orion and Perseus didn't have anything to do with what happened to me."

"You can't know that."

"Not unless we talk to them."

"Why do you think they would talk to you when they're not talking to anyone else?"

"Because I'm charming?"

Leon stared at Callum. Callum stared back, not one bit intimidated. He wasn't useless or powerless. He might not be able to fight as well as Leon, or at all, really, but that didn't mean there was nothing he could do to help.

He chose his next words carefully because he didn't want to offend Leon or for him to dismiss what he was saying. "You and the other mutants have been through horrific things that no one should ever live through. You survived, and you're incredibly strong. Going through all that gave you a thirst for revenge, though, and sometimes, you have a hard time seeing past that. I think that this situation is one of those times."

"We don't want revenge on Perseus and Orion. We just want to know what they know," Leon pointed out.

"You want to know what they know because you think it'll take you to other hunters and labs."

"That's what we do. We find labs and free people. We find hunters and get rid of them before they can get rid of us."

"Because you want all of them to pay for what they did."

"We're in this to save people."

Leon sounded hurt, which meant Callum was messing this up.

"I know that's your main goal, and it's admirable. I wish I could do what you do, but I don't think I'll ever be able to stomach it. As good as you are at raiding labs and all of that, I think that in this situation, you need a softer touch. Perseus and Orion are probably terrified. We don't even know they're hunters for sure because they won't talk."

"What else could they be?"

"We won't find out if this continues, Leon. Unless Moore changes something, he won't get anything from them. That's why I think that sending someone else would help. Change things up. Show them that you're not planning to hurt them. Explain that you want answers and that you'll let them go when you have them."

"We won't," Leon whispered.

It was almost as if he was afraid that Callum would freak out when he found out, but Callum already knew they wouldn't let the brothers go. They hadn't let the other hunter go, either. Callum didn't know any details, and he wasn't planning to ask, but he knew he'd been killed.

Callum didn't feel sorry. The man had hit him with a baseball bat. He'd hurt him, and he could have killed him. He probably wouldn't have cared. Perseus and Orion were different. Yes, Perseus had kidnapped Leon, but he'd done so for his brother. Leon was the best healer in the village, and somehow, it seemed that Perseus had known that.

Callum wanted to know how.

Leon should continue to tell Callum it was a bad idea, because it was. Callum wasn't trained for any of this, and the brothers could be dangerous. From what Leon knew, they hadn't been aggressive or anything like that, but he didn't want to risk it.

He didn't want to risk his mate.

But something told him that if he said that Callum's plan wasn't going to happen, Callum would find a way to make it work. He'd go behind Leon's back, and that might be even more dangerous than doing this in the open. Callum was stubborn, and Leon wasn't willing to put him in danger.

Of course, he wouldn't be the one making the decision. It would be Moore, and Leon suspected his answer would be no. Still, if Callum wanted to ask him, then he should. That way he'd know where he stood.

"All right," Leon said with a sigh. "We can talk to Moore. Don't be surprised when he says no, though."

Callum bounced a little. "Why would he say no?"

"Because the brothers are hunters, which means they're dangerous, and you're not trained. Even if you were, there's a reason Moore is the only one interrogating them. The less they know about us, the better."

"They already know about me," Callum pointed out. "I was there when we rescued you, remember?"

"You didn't rescue me," Leon muttered.

"I don't know about that. I mean, you were kidnapped. We found you and took you home, so it feels like we did rescue you."

"You can't rescue me when I'm not in danger."

"So you admit you were never in danger and that the brothers are harmless?"

"I'm not admitting to anything, and I don't think they're harmless." They were hiding something, and Leon wanted to know what that was.

The hunters weren't usually like this. They were harder, in-your-face bigots and never hesitated to scream at Moore and insult him. The slurs Leon had heard would make anybody's skin crawl, and he'd expected the brothers to behave that way. They hadn't, which made them a bit of a mystery, and since, for now, Leon didn't have anything else to do, he wanted to try to unravel it. Besides, Moore was stretching his time as much as he could, but between interrogating the brothers and planning the raid against the lab they'd found after the accident, he barely had any time for himself and his mate. Maybe he'd be relieved that someone else could take over the interrogations.

Leon hauled himself off the couch. Callum was next to him instantly, and he looked as though Leon was taking him to Disneyland rather than to a damp cell to interrogate a prisoner. Leon almost rolled his eyes, but he didn't want Callum to think he was making fun of him. He wasn't. He found Callum's excitement endearing, as he did the fact that Callum seemed to believe the brothers were good people.

As far as Leon was concerned, no hunter was good. He didn't care what happened to these two. He was curious, but it wouldn't change the way he felt or thought about them.

They were hunters, and eventually, they'd try to kill them. Even if they didn't, they'd already done horrible things they needed to pay for. Leon didn't have the same faith Callum had that everything would be all right because he already knew that wouldn't be the case.

But he didn't want to take the smile away from Callum's face, so instead of cautioning him, he followed him outside. They headed to Moore's place, and Callum took the lead, which was a relief. Moore might yell at Leon for wanting to do such a stupid thing, but he wouldn't yell at Callum. Callum was too cute, and Moore didn't know him well, so he wouldn't want to scare him.

Callum knocked on the door, and when Moore opened it, he beamed at him. Moore seemed taken aback and blinked, then looked at Leon as if asking what was going on.

Leon sighed. "Callum wants to talk to you."

"Yeah? Well, come on in. Tell me what I can do for you."

"You can let us talk to the constellation brothers," Callum said, going straight to the point.

Moore blinked at him again. This time, he looked like he was trying to make sense of the words.

"You mean the hunter brothers?"

"Yes. Why is everyone asking me that? Who else do you think I'd be talking about?"

"Why would you want to talk to them? They kidnapped your mate."

"You don't have to remind me of that. I'm well aware of what they did, as I am of the fact that only Perseus kidnapped him. It feels kind of unfair that you're also keeping Orion in a cell."

Moore crossed his arms over his chest. He didn't ask them if they wanted to sit down or if they wanted something to eat. Instead, he stared at Callum as if he was trying to make sense of him.

"I'm listening," he said.

Callum seemed to think that was a good thing, and his

smile stayed on his lips. "How long have you been talking to them?"

"Since they arrived."

"And what did you get from those conversations? Do we know more than their names? Maybe what they were doing in the area, or how they know about the village?"

"Orion is still confused about how they got here, so he wasn't able to tell me anything. Perseus has refused to talk to me."

"Did he say why?"

"No, and frankly, I don't care. If he ever wants to get out of that cell, he's going to have to tell me what they were doing here."

"Maybe he's afraid of you. Maybe that's why he's not talking."

"Of course he's afraid of me. I'm a shifter."

"You're also kind of intimidating, so it's possible *that's* why Perseus won't talk to you. I think you should let someone else try. What you're doing isn't working, and it's time to try something else."

Moore looked at Leon. "You agree?"

"He's not wrong when he says that nothing you've done has helped," Leon pointed out, hoping Moore wouldn't kick his ass. "I don't know if he can get any more answers than you did from them, but it's worth trying."

"Actually, I thought that you should be the one to talk to them," Callum interjected.

Leon really didn't want to do it, but at the same time, he was curious about the brothers and wanted to give Callum everything he could ever want.

Including a conversation with two hunter brothers, who might be plotting to kill them right at this moment.

"Do you think that since Leon saved Orion, Perseus would be open to talking to him rather than me?" Moore asked.

Dammit. He sounded interested and like he was considering it, which Leon hadn't expected. He'd thought Moore would tell Callum it wasn't possible and send him on his way, not that he'd actually get him to the cells to talk to the brothers.

"Maybe," Callum answered. "At the very least, it's worth a try. Perseus got what he wanted. His brother is healthy, and even though they're both stuck in a cell, they're fine. From what little I saw of him, his brother is his entire world, and he'd do anything to protect him." He looked sideways at Leon. "Maybe that's something else Leon can use to get answers. He understands wanting to protect a younger brother."

Leon didn't want to talk about his brother with two hunters, but he didn't have to give them details or a name. He didn't like the sound of any of this, but they needed answers, and this might be the only way to get them. They had to find out what the hunters were doing and what they were planning on next. They had to know who knew about the village and what they would do with that information.

And apparently, Leon was the only one who might be able to get the answers to all those questions.

Callum tried to stay quiet as they walked toward the cells. He didn't want Moore to change his mind and was afraid to ask Leon what he thought of all of this.

He hadn't expected Moore to agree to have both him and Leon there. He wanted to talk to the brothers and ask Perseus why he'd kidnapped Leon instead of talking to him, but he hadn't thought he'd have the opportunity to do so. Leon was protective of him, almost too much, and he'd expected Moore to be the same.

Instead, Moore had agreed almost instantly. Leon had

looked like he wanted to argue, but thankfully, he hadn't, although he didn't look happy. Callum almost expected him to change his mind and tell Moore neither of them was doing this, but he didn't try to stop them, not even when they reached a small cement building at the edge of the village.

The cells.

The village didn't have a proper jail or anything like that. Even when they had hunters, they didn't keep them long. Depending on what information the hunters gave them and what they agreed to, they were either taken care of or handed over to the council. Callum hoped the brothers wouldn't be killed. Something told him there was more to their story than what he knew, and he wanted to find out what that more was.

That was why he was here, ignoring how his mate glared at him. He followed Moore inside the small building. The first room held a table and a few chairs, a couple of them occupied by guards, but another door opened on a short hallway. That was where the cells were, and Callum swallowed. He was suddenly nervous, even though he knew the brothers were the only hunters here. The man who'd hurt him was long gone, and Callum would never see him again.

Moore didn't step into the hallway with them. Instead, he moved to the side of the door and gestured at Callum to walk in. Callum wasn't surprised when Leon moved in front of him. Of course he'd want to make sure it was safe before he allowed Callum anywhere near the brothers.

"Finally," a voice said.

Something moved in one of the cells, and Perseus appeared at the bars. He looked from Leon to Moore, then apparently decided that he didn't care that Moore was watching him. He leaned closer to the bars but didn't reach between them to touch Leon. That was good because Callum was pretty sure Leon would have torn his hand off if he had.

"I wanted to apologize for what I did," Perseus quickly

said.

Moore snorted. "That's more than I've ever heard from him, so I'll leave you to it. I'll be right behind the door."

Callum nodded. His mouth was dry, and he had no idea what he was supposed to do. Maybe the first thing was to introduce himself.

He could only imagine how confusing the situation had to be for the brothers, especially Orion. They had no idea where they were, who had taken them, and why. Although maybe that wasn't quite so. If they knew about Fairview, they had to know who lived there and what they did.

"I'm Callum," he said, moving deeper into the hallway.

Perseus's cell was on the left, while Orion was in the cell on the right. He'd been lying stretched out on the tiny bed, but now he sat up. He appeared as curious as Callum to hear what Leon and Perseus were saying.

"I'm Orion," Orion said.

Callum nodded at him, then turned to Perseus. "And I already know your name."

"Who are you?" Perseus asked as he crossed his arms over his chest and took a step back.

"Leon's mate."

Perseus's scowl vanished. "I'm really sorry about what I did. I shouldn't have kidnapped him."

"Damn right you shouldn't have," Leon snapped. "It was the stupidest thing you could have done."

Callum didn't want the situation to degenerate, so he quickly stepped in. He should have predicted that Leon would be too angry to do a good job. "I understand why you panicked, and I think Leon does, too. You were scared for your brother, and you did the only thing you could think of through the panic."

Leon sucked in a breath. He took a few seconds to gather himself, and he appeared calmer by the time he looked at

Perseus again. "I might have done the same if it had been my brother in Orion's condition. It would have been better if you'd talked to me, but I do understand why you didn't."

Perseus's shoulders slumped. "Thank God." He and Orion exchanged a glance. "My brother is all right now, right? You're not here because he needs more healing."

"He's as healthy as he was before he got injured. I'm here because you haven't been answering Moore's questions. We want to know more about you and what happened to you and find out how you know about Fairview."

"I want to know if you're hunters," Callum said. As far as he knew, no one had actually asked them. They'd all assumed the brothers were hunters, but they didn't look like the kind of people Callum imagined hunters would be.

The guy who'd attacked him had been angry and hadn't hesitated to hit him. He would have killed him if he hadn't given him what he wanted, but neither of these two would do something like that. Callum was sure of it, even though he didn't know them.

Perseus sighed and went to sit on the bed in his cell. "I guess we are."

"I thought that was a question you'd answer with a yes or a no." Callum had no idea what *I guess we are* meant.

"We were never good hunters," Orion explained. "Our father is a rabid hunter. He believes shifters and any kind of supernatural creature deserve to die, and if he can make any money out of that, he's happy. He's been raising us in that life since we were kids, but back then, the organization was much smaller. Then, a few years ago, they allied with the labs and the people who created them."

"Orion . . ." Perseus started.

Orion shook his head. "I'm done with this. I'm done with *him*. I don't care what he wants for us or from us. It's not what *I* want to do with my life. I don't want to hurt people."

112

Perseus stared at him for a moment before nodding. "All right." He turned to Leon. "Can you promise my brother won't be hurt?"

"I can," Leon confirmed. "Unless he attacks someone, no one here will hurt him or you."

"Orion was injured because he tried to stop another hunter. We've been trying to do that for years. Once we realized what the hunters had started doing with the labs, we freed as many people as we could after they were kidnapped. Unfortunately, it wasn't nearly enough, but we tried."

"You could have left," Leon pointed out.

"With what money? We've worked with our father since we were teenagers, and he's the only one who gets paid. He gets everything, and he feeds and houses us." Perseus snorted. "If we can even call it that. We both wanted to leave for a long time, but we didn't have a choice unless we wanted to be homeless. The few times we tried to run anyway, our father beat Orion so badly that he could barely walk, let alone survive without a roof over his head or food. I couldn't go on my own and leave him there, so I stayed, too."

"We both did," Orion murmured. "But we should have done more. We should have chosen to be homeless. I just thought we were doing enough good."

Callum wanted to hug the big guy. Even though Orion was bigger, he gave the impression of being softer and so gentle that it made Callum's heart hurt. "Are you willing to give us names and places?" he asked. "I don't know what's going to happen to you, but if you give Moore and the others what they want, they might be able to help. We only want to protect our people. That's why we need more details about the hunters."

"And we need to know how you knew about Fairview," Leon added.

"One of the people we helped escape told me about it,"

Orion explained. "It sounded like it was too good to be true. She said that if we wanted to leave the hunters, the leader of this village would help us."

From what little Callum knew about Rikar, he just might. Callum hoped he would because even though these two were hunters, it was clear their hearts had never been into it. They'd been with the hunters for a long time, though, so they had enough information to help keep Fairview safe and finally completely get rid of the hunters.

And maybe even the labs.

CHAPTER SEVEN

Leon felt like he was about to jump out of his skin. He couldn't remember the last time he'd been so excited and, at the same time, worried.

He still wasn't sure this was the right way to do this. Maybe he should have called his parents and told them he was alive instead of appearing on their doorstep with Teddy. He wasn't sure they'd have believed him, and he was terrified that they might say they didn't want to see him.

So shimmering in front of their house it would be.

Thankfully, Leon wouldn't be going alone. Of course, Teddy was needed for the shimmering part, but Callum would also be there. He'd promised Leon he'd stay with him for as long as he needed him, and if he wanted some privacy with his family, Callum was willing to give him that, too. He didn't understand that he was part of the family, but that was all right. As soon as Leon's parents learned that Callum was his mate, they'd make him feel welcome, and he'd finally understand.

"You're pretty bouncy," Callum gently teased.

"I learned from the best of them," Leon said as he hooked an arm around Callum's shoulders.

He pulled his mate close to kiss the top of his head. Callum snuggled against him, only to push away when someone knocked on their door.

Teddy had arrived.

Leon followed Callum to the front door. Sure enough, Teddy was there, and he was smiling. He appeared genuinely happy to be doing this for Leon, but the smile didn't reach his eyes for some reason.

Something had been wrong with him for a while now. Leon was pretty sure it had started when he'd been kidnapped, and he couldn't help but wonder if Teddy had been that scared for him. Was this what it felt like to be on the other side of things? Leon had been terrified for his friends before, and now, it seemed Teddy was afraid for him.

But he was fine. He hadn't been hurt, and the hunters who had grabbed him weren't even good hunters. As soon as Callum had explained to Perseus and Orion what he wanted, both of them had blurted out everything they knew. Moore had been so excited that he'd almost smiled, which was something that usually only happened when his mate was around.

So far, they hadn't done anything with the information. They had to be careful, especially because Orion had warned them that their father knew they weren't happy as hunters. He believed his father would be too proud to admit that they would betray him and the others, but it was something they needed to keep in mind. Besides, this was a too big operation for the mutants to do it on their own. Moore had called the council assassins, and they were still trying to find a way to make it work. They had enough information to take down most of the hunters. They had the location of several of the labs and details of what was being done inside those buildings. It was a lot, but they could finally stop raiding lab by lab and actually make a difference, and in the end, that was all that mattered.

Well, that and seeing his family again.

"Ready?" Teddy asked.

"I don't think I've ever been more ready."

"He woke up at five this morning, and he was already like this," Callum said.

Teddy nodded. "It's understandable."

Leon was tempted to grab Teddy's hand and get it over with, but it was clear his friend wasn't feeling well. "We can do this another time if you're not up to it," he said gently.

"I'm not letting you go another time. I'm fine." Teddy sounded almost offended.

"You haven't looked fine in a while," Callum pointed out. "We truly can wait. It's not like they're expecting us."

"Leon has been waiting for this for a long time. I'm not going to keep him away from his family just because of my personal problems."

So there *was* something. "We're your friends," Leon said. "I know you don't want to take away from this day, but it doesn't have to be that way. I'm seeing my family again, but remember that you're my family, too. How am I supposed to focus on my parents and brother when I'm worried about you?"

Teddy's eyes narrowed, but eventually, he sighed, and his shoulders slumped. "You know where to hit to hurt me," he muttered.

"Because you're my best friend. I don't want to hurt you, though. I want to help you hurt less."

"It's nothing I need your help with. I don't think you could help even if you tried, which is why I didn't tell anyone. Well, that, and because everyone has been busy, and you were thinking about your family. You already have enough on your plate."

Leon stared because he knew nothing he could say would rush Teddy into telling them whatever was happening.

He wanted to grab his hand and see his parents and his little brother, but he hadn't been lying when he'd said that Teddy was just as important. Leon wasn't abandoning his new family for his old one. He wouldn't be leaving Fairview or anyone behind. His heart had enough space to love everyone, including Teddy.

Teddy raked a hand through his hair, then smoothed it down. "Have you seen the brothers lately?"

"We talked to them yesterday," Callum answered. "They seem to enjoy our company."

Or rather, Perseus was still trying to get Leon to forgive him for what he'd done. It didn't matter that Leon had already explained he didn't hold it against him and that he understood what Perseus had been going through. Every time they saw each other, the first thing Perseus said was *I'm sorry*.

"They're okay? Both of them?"

"Yeah. Moore and Rikar have been talking about letting them out eventually."

Teddy sucked in a breath and nodded. "Good. Will you tell me when they're allowed to leave the cells?"

"I'm pretty sure everyone in the village will know. What's going on, Teddy?"

It was good to see that Callum cared about Leon's friends as much as Leon did. Teddy hadn't told Leon about any of this, but maybe he'd tell Callum. They were friends. Their friendship was different than the friendship between Teddy and Leon, but it didn't mean it was weaker. They shared different experiences, and that was all right.

"It's Perseus," Teddy eventually said. "He's my mate, and I have no idea how to deal with that. I don't know if I can."

Leon gaped. That was the last thing he'd expected to hear, and if he'd been in Teddy's place, he would have been freaking out, too.

But not Callum. Callum didn't freak out and didn't say anything that would offend Teddy, like asking him how it was possible or saying he was sorry for the mistake Fate had made. Not that Leon felt that way. He was shocked and knew it would be better if he kept his mouth shut.

"Oh, Teddy," Callum murmured. "It's all right. He's not a bad person."

"He's a hunter."

"Haven't you heard the entire story? He was forced to work as a hunter, but he and his brother did everything they could to help people and keep them safe. They've paid for that time and time again in blood, but now, they're out. They've been helping us and giving us information because they want the hunters to be defeated. They never wanted to hurt anyone. They just wanted to survive and did so the only way they knew how to."

Leon could understand that, and he suspected Teddy could, too. Leon had done things he wasn't proud of when he'd been in the lab, and the memories still tormented him, but he didn't regret what he'd done. He'd been trying to survive, and he had.

Just like Perseus and Orion. Just like Teddy.

"I don't know what to do," Teddy admitted.

"Whatever your heart wants," Leon said before Callum could answer. "You don't have to stay away from him just because of what he was before. If you want to be careful, then be careful, but don't close your heart to him. You'll regret it, and I don't want you to feel that way for any reason."

Teddy nodded. "I'm not giving up. It's just a mess."

"Good thing we're used to messes, then, right?" Leon's life had been a mess, but he was finally on the other side of it. He had his mate, a job he wanted to do, and now, he was getting his family back. He wished everyone could be as happy as he was.

Especially Teddy.

ABOUT THE AUTHOR

Catherine is the creator of several series, most of them paranormal, including the Whitedell Pride Series and the Gillham Pack Series. While she graduated in translation, she decided to go the writer's way because it was more fun to create her own stories and characters.

She's been living in Italy for more than twenty years, but she's a daughter of the North—Belgium to be precise—and she misses it so much that she's already planning to move back.

She loves pizza—probably too much—her son, her pets, and of course, books. She sneaks some reading time into her schedule every time she has five minutes free from writing, demands from her various pets and son, and lastly, housework.

Connect with her:

lievens.catherine@gmail.com
BookBub: https://www.bookbub.com/authors/catherine-lievens
Website: https://authorcatherinelievens.com/
Facebook: https://www.facebook.com/catherine.lievens.9
Facebook Group: https://www.facebook.com/groups/411788002341528/
Twitter: https://twitter.com/authorCLievens
Newsletter: http://eepurl.com/c-uvKn